1. Tu

I was tempted to start this off by telling you I have a good sense of humour. That I like fun, travel and adventure and hope to meet someone similar for friendship, possibly more. But that would have given completely the wrong idea about my connection with the dating agency. Plus only the first bit is true. Although I'd been single for quite a while, my involvement with the *Kisses and Cuddles* dating agency was entirely professional.

I'm a computer programmer and website creator, and yes, I'm aware I don't fit the stereotype. People expect a boy, barely past his teens, hiding behind glasses, the name of an obscure fantasy film character, and all black clothing. I'm thirty-two, dress normally and use the name Willow only because it's on my birth certificate. I'm not a numbers obsessed loner either; I've had boyfriends. We'd always had plenty in common. Perhaps too much as we spent most of our time talking about code and broadband speeds or debating the merits of Flash over HTML 5. Frankly I got enough of that in the hours I was paid to think about it.

Although I advertise for programming work, I'd mostly only had boring jobs updating existing websites, so I was a bit surprised to be asked to write a programme to match up the dating agency's romantic hopefuls. The *Kisses and Cuddles* office is quite near my home, so I walked round there. My neighbour would be pleased if he knew; Craig's always telling me I don't need the car for short trips. He's a bit of a nag, but also right – I really should try to get more exercise.

Maybe I should have been better prepared for the owner o f *Kisses and Cuddles* not fitting my preconceived ideas. She isn't some romantic, cat loving old lady. Nor is she a hard-hearted cynic in a power suit and killer heels. Norbert is just a regular businessman; not cold and calculating when compared with my other clients, but his attitude seemed a bit that way for dealing with romance. He's tall, dark, and if you like that brooding Poldark sort of look, I guess you'd consider him attractive.

Almost the first thing he did was to name the rather low fee he was willing to pay. "I'm just starting up and it's all I can afford, just now."

I appreciated him coming to the point and I believed him. I'd struggled to get going when I started my own business. Actually the struggle was ongoing. "I can probably do it for that amount if it's nothing too complicated," I said.

"I'm not technologically minded enough to be sure, but I think and hope it's straightforward. Would you like tea or coffee?"

He had a tiny fridge and kettle in his office, so accepting wouldn't waste much of our time. "Tea please. Plenty of milk and two sugars."

He placed my tea and his black coffee on the desk, then took a box of biscuits out of his desk. "Sorry, there are only those strange pink wafers left."

"My favourite." I took three. As I saw it, if he didn't like them, I was doing him a favour.

A subtle buzzer sounded.

"Will you excuse me a moment, Willow. It seems I may have a client."

Love Is The Answer

Patsy Collins

To my wee mate Dawn Brown –
for providing more than one answer and a
fair amount of cake!

Contents

As Norbert left the office, I couldn't resist a glance after him into the tiny reception area. Looking uncomfortable in the tiny space was a stocky, blond man who looked familiar. Probably just my imagination though. All that pink upholstery, swirly wallpaper and floral displays would make anyone's eyes glad of something a bit plainer to look at.

Norbert was soon back. "Sorry about that. Thankfully I've been able to increase my receptionist's hours and she'll be full-time from next week." He took a sip of his coffee. "I promise that if you take on this job and my business is successful I'll hire you for any future computer work I require."

I decided I'd probably take the job. A repeat client would be good – if Norbert kept his word. "So, if you could run through your requirements?" I invited.

"I need a way to collect the personal details both of each client, and the person they'd like to meet, and to match up those people with an appropriate percentage of compatibility."

"Just standard data gathering and a mathematical calculation?" I asked. That would be dull, but easy.

"Exactly."

"And what percentage of compatibility do you consider acceptable to create matches?"

"Sixty-seven."

"Why?" It seemed an odd figure.

"It's high enough that the clients will have enough things in common, not so high that there would be too few matches to make the business viable. And it's my door number." He told me he'd been working out the matches himself so far, but could no longer keep up so needed a programme. That made me feel more optimistic about the repeat business.

"I notice you don't wear a wedding ring. If you're single I'd like to offer you free membership," Norbert said.

I declined that. Call me a romantic, but I wanted to meet someone by chance as though we were made for each other, not as the result of an algorithm.

I left with a contract, warm handshake and the list of questions clients were asked. That was all fine in theory, but lots of the boxes were for things such as height or eye colour. I wasn't convinced most people looking for love would be so shallow that if a person was an inch shorter than they'd requested, or had honey rather than caramel coloured eyes, they wouldn't be interested. I adjusted the calculations so that physical attributes would have less influence than interests and personality traits. Even so I wasn't satisfied. In real life people with apparently little in common are often thrown together and get on surprisingly well.

When I got home again, my neighbour Craig's bicycle was still in our shared hallway, so it probably wasn't him I'd seen at *Kisses and Cuddles*. Like me he often works from home. I'd have invited him in for a mug of tea if I hadn't just had one. We take our breaks together a couple of times a week to make a change from working alone. Usually that happens when we don't actually have much work to do and right then I had.

I decided to build some randomness into the selection programme. Not too much. Most would be calculated mathematically, with those having a minimum 67% compatibility rating being matched. Then every Tuesday there would be a wild card. I retained a few checks. Vegetarians wouldn't be partnered with butchers and those with violently opposing political opinions would be kept apart, and they'd have to have a minimum 11% compatibility rating. Other than that, two people would be matched entirely at random. Eleven is my door number, in case you are wondering.

When I visited Norbert to deliver my work, I walked again. I was already feeling, and I hoped looking, fitter. I'd taken extra care to dress nicely. Anyone who saw me there might mistake me for a client and I didn't want to harm his business by looking like an undesirable date. I very much wanted *Kisses and Cuddles* to be a success and generate further work for me.

When I was greeted by Clare, Norbert's receptionist, I was glad I'd made an effort. She was pretty and stylish enough for me to want to hate her, yet so charming I just couldn't. Although I'm not exactly hideous, I'm no looker compared with her. Even so Clare didn't make the obvious assumption that I was a prospective client, instead simply asked how she could help me.

Norbert again made tea for me and coffee for himself. This time his biscuit tin contained a wider selection, but still included my favourite pink wafers. We spent a while testing the system. First by putting in our genuine details and requesting a match. Despite us being the only two entries on the new system at that stage, the computer didn't pair us up. Naturally I'd taken the precaution not to try this on a Tuesday, and as we're very different in many ways we didn't reach the 67% compatibility rating. Actually it was barely half of that.

Next Norbert transferred in the data from his most recent

clients and was soon able to print out a selection of possible matches for each of them. He appeared very pleased with what I'd done, although I did wonder if he suspected I'd exceeded my brief, as a couple of times it seemed as though he was about to say something, but changed his mind.

A couple of weeks later I had a call from Norbert and was initially concerned that he might have realised what I'd done, especially as he was calling on a Tuesday. I needn't have worried, it was just a courtesy call to say my programme was running well, that he'd paid my invoice, and to reassure me that he'd offer me any further computer work he might require in the future.

I started getting much more business after that. My neighbour Craig put some work my way and several new customers said Norbert had recommended me. That was a form of matchmaking I definitely approved of. Other than a few emails, I didn't hear from Norbert until he asked me to come in and discuss the possibility of creating a brand new website for *Kisses and Cuddles*. Again I dressed in clothes which I hoped wouldn't scare off any of Norbert's clients I might happen to meet.

"What a lovely blouse," Clare said. "That colour is perfect for you, Willow."

"Thank you. Have you had your hair done?"

"How sweet of you to notice!"

Norbert must have overheard our conversation as he told Clare her new hairstyle looked nice. To be fair, they might have been too busy for him to have had the chance to remark on it before, but as it was three in the afternoon, I'm not absolutely sure that was the case.

"I'm delighted with what you've done for me so far," Norbert said as he made my tea just the way I like it. "And as you know, technology isn't really my thing, so I'm relying on you to guide me."

After agreeing the routine stuff, such as a contact page, data input and payment sections I made suggestions. "You could feature some of the couples you've successfully matched, if you think they'd be agreeable."

"Good idea, Willow. I've had lots of thank you letters, so I think some might be willing to do that."

He told me about some of the happy relationships which had started thanks to *Kisses and Cuddles*.

"I believe you, Norbert, but I still don't want to sign up."

"I didn't mean… I'm sure you already have someone special in your life."

I'm not sure why, but I admitted that wasn't the case. "I've been so busy lately that I really only meet people through work and so far none of them have… "

"Been over 67% compatible?" he suggested.

"Exactly."

Norbert called me a few days later to say he'd obtained photographs and quotes from happy clients and asked me to come in.

"No need, you can just email it over."

"There's another matter that I'd like to speak to you about in person."

Clearly his business was doing well as not only could be afford the new website, but he had to reject several of the dates I suggested for the meeting.

Norbert greeted me just as warmly as before. "When I went through the lists of people who'd notified us that they'd begun relationships with their dates, I found a few anomalies." He passed me a photo of a statuesque blonde and a short, tubby man of about the same age. At their feet were three labradors.

To gain thinking time, I ate a couple of the pink wafer biscuits. "It says they've got engaged," I pointed out. The couple looked so happy that I was keen to put that image on the website.

"Yes, that's good but very surprising news." He pushed two profiles towards me. "He was looking for someone short, dark and mature with a liking for cats. She hoped to meet someone younger and sporty."

"It says here he plays… oh, chess." I was beginning to think they might not be such a good advert – and was certain they'd both signed up on the same Tuesday.

"Thankfully they're delighted with the services of *Kisses and Cuddles*." Norbert shrugged. "And there's these two." He indicated a photo of two women. "Chris and Pat both declared they wanted to meet men, so naturally assumed the system would match them with someone male. Both have small children who demand a lot of attention, so didn't realise the other was female until they arrived at the restaurant."

"Ah." It seemed my Tuesday wildcard matches were a little more random than I'd intended.

"They decided that as they'd gone to the trouble of getting baby sitters and dressing up, they'd share a meal anyway. They realised sympathetic company was what they'd really wanted, and have become good friends, so although they suggested the blip in the system be investigated they didn't want their money back."

"Well, that's good."

"Hmm. And here we have two widowers who were matched up and have also became friends. They assure me they had a good laugh about it and their friendship has stopped their kids worrying about them and pushing them into trying again."

Those three were the most extreme, but he'd uncovered more happy couples whose compatibility rating shouldn't have allowed them to be paired up. "It's happened once a week since you installed the programme and always on a Tuesday."

He was easily intelligent enough to work out this was no coincidence, so I decided to confess. "I'm sorry, but sticking so rigidly to mathematical calculations just didn't seem romantic and well, that didn't feel right. If you'll give me another chance, I promise I'll fix it."

"No. You took a liberty with my programming."

What he said was true, but I'd thought from his tone earlier on that I'd been forgiven for my silly, romantic addition. I'd even started to convince myself that not all his clients hated pink wafers and he'd actually saved some just for me. Now it seemed I was going to lose not only the new business I'd been promised but my existing contract too.

"And I've done the same with these." He showed me the forms we'd each completed the day I'd demonstrated my system for matching couples.

"You've put me onto the database?"

"No. Us. Want to wait whilst I run today's matches?"

Of course I did; haven't I proved I'm a romantic? While the programme ran, it occurred to me that Norbert and I had met pretty much by chance, had very little in common. I also realised it was a Tuesday.

As I said, I'd have liked to start this by telling you I have a good sense of humour. That I like fun, travel and adventure and hope to meet someone similar for friendship, possibly more. That would give the wrong impression though. You see I'm no longer single. In fact a photo of Norbert and myself feature on the success stories page of the *Kisses and Cuddles* lovely new website.

Oh sorry, I've jumped ahead a bit and missed telling you about the reports, haven't I? When the computer beeped to say it had created matches, Norbert just stared at the computer. You know the look actors in the old silent films used to show they were horrified? Well, he was doing that.

I didn't want to ask, but eventually I had to. "Another blip?"

Norbert turned the screen towards me. The profiles which showed an 11% compatibility match belonged to his receptionist Clare and my neighbour Craig. They're both really nice people, but…

I reached across and squeezed Norbert's hand. Then I pressed the delete key. "Run it again tomorrow," I said.

He did. Norbert and Clare were almost perfectly matched at 92% compatibility. Craig and I are one better at 93%. I'll leave you to work out which couple are having a swirly, pink and floral themed wedding.

2. Always Adamant

"I see you've pencilled in to take this Saturday off," Tanya's colleague said as she waited for a client's perm to take.

"Yes, that's right."

"You don't have definite plans to go somewhere do you?"

"Not exactly." Tanya's husband had dropped something of a bombshell, which she needed to discuss with him, but she hadn't yet worked out precisely how, or when, to tackle that.

"It's just that I've been offered the chance of an adventure weekend in the Lake District. It's going to be amazing." The younger woman spoke enthusiastically about visiting an area she'd never been to before and how much she enjoyed water sports.

Before Tanya realised quite what was happening, she'd been talked out of her Saturday off. Her own fault for being so indecisive.

She was grateful her husband didn't push her around like that but it didn't make her decision about whether to stay or go any easier. The cancelled day off did help with planning their conversation though. It would have to be Sunday after their children had been and gone. As Tanya rinsed the client's hair, she let her mind wander, in the hope it would settle on an answer.

A few days previously she'd seen her husband reading what was almost certainly an old letter. Like her he was just about to turn fifty and thinking back to his youth. He'd rummaged through the loft and shown her several mementoes from the early days of their relationship and his childhood. She'd been prompted to dig out her old diaries and found the one from 1981. She hadn't written much on each page, because she hadn't needed to.

No teenage angst for Tanya. She used to be so sure about everything back then. Not always right, but invariably absolutely sure. She was going to have an amazing life full of travel, adventure and fun. Nothing ordinary. For a while she'd been totally in love with the singer Adam Ant. She'd liked other stars too, but she positively knew she'd forever be the Goody Two Shoes to Adam's Prince Charming.

She'd probably also known even then that a relationship between them wouldn't have worked, even if by some remote chance it had got started. That didn't matter though because Paul was in her English class. The teacher got them to try putting forward arguments for causes they didn't believe in. Tanya couldn't remember why or what he'd discussed, but she did remember a class mate saying "Are you sure?"

"Yes," Paul had replied confidently. "I'm adamant."

For a moment she'd thought he was claiming to be Adam Ant. Until then she'd taken very little notice of Paul. Those words changed all that and she soon saw he was funny, kind and shared her adventurous spirit. It took very little effort to persuade Paul to ask her out.

Tanya's life hadn't always been easy, but once she made up her mind she wanted something she worked hard to achieve her aim and generally got there. She'd persuaded someone to take her on for the job she wanted in the hairdressing salon and train her to do it. She'd had the wedding and the children and the house. They'd needed to work long hours, and the children had attended after-school clubs, Brownies and Scouts and visited friends almost as much as they'd been home, but she'd been sure they were doing the right thing. They had done the right thing. The children were happy and confident and now led independent, fulfilled lives. The mortgage was paid off on their nice sensible little house in a pleasant area. She still had her job too. And her marriage.

But… there was something missing. It was all so ordinary. No, that wasn't the problem. She'd grown up since she was fourteen. There was nothing wrong with ordinary if that's what she now wanted. The trouble was, she didn't know. That certainty was gone. Had been gone even before she realised her husband wasn't satisfied with things as they were.

Tanya might not have been convinced her ordinary, safe home and slightly dull routine were exactly what she wanted, but she was even less sure that she wanted to give them up. She didn't want to lose her husband either, but if he wasn't willing to stay she didn't have much choice.

Her client expressed delight in the finished hairstyle and tipped generously. "And thanks for letting me talk through my problems, it's really helped."

Tanya hadn't actually done anything other than encourage the woman to express her concerns as her new curls were blow-dried. She hadn't even really listened. Perhaps seeing the answer was as simple as clearly seeing the problem.

After work Tanya dug out more diaries. In one she'd written page after page about the exciting things she and Paul would do. Their plan had been to earn some money, then back-pack around the world. In many of the entries she'd sounded very like her enthusiastic colleague had when she'd managed to wangle the day off simply by being so clear about wanting it. According to another diary Tanya had been in love with a boy called Jeremy who she couldn't remember, Tim who she could, and Jed who was best forgotten. She'd been decisive all right – until the moment she abruptly altered course. Some things had stayed with her though, including her liking for Adam Ant's music… which she could hear now.

She'd been so engrossed in her reading she hadn't noticed her husband come home and put the stereo on. He handed her a glass of wine.

"Trying to soften me up?" she asked.

"No, but I do want us to talk."

It was Wednesday night and she'd planned their discussion for Sunday, but now was the right time; she knew it.

"I don't think I explained myself very well," he began. "I have been thinking about turning fifty and read some old letters, but this isn't a sudden whim or midlife crisis."

"I know," Tanya said.

"You do?"

"Yes, you've been feeling a bit unsettled for a long time. Unsure, indecisive, not knowing if you're doing the right thing."

"Yes. How did you… you too?"

"Yes, Paul. Me too. But I'm not the girl who wrote you those letters about the travelling we'd do, the adventures we'd have."

"Yes you are."

Was he right? Tanya would like to think so. "Well, maybe a bit, but not just her. I'm sensible now. I see the advantages of a proper home, a guaranteed income, and there's the children to consider. We can't just sell up and back-pack around the world for the rest of our lives."

"No, we can't."

"No?" Tanya demanded. He was really going to go ahead without her?

"Sorry, I was so pleased to be sure what I wanted once again that I didn't properly explain. I'm not talking about selling up. I thought we'd let out the house, take a sabbatical from work and get a campervan. Tour Europe for a year."

"Oh!"

Tanya's first reaction was a decisive gut instinct. Once that would have been enough for her to know how to reply, but she forced herself to think carefully first. She'd miss the children and wasn't overly keen on having strangers living in her house. But the internet would keep her family in touch, they could redecorate when they returned and she'd be welcomed back at work. More importantly they'd have the adventure they'd always wanted, her and Paul together.

"OK then, let's do that," Tanya said.

"You're sure?" Paul asked.

"Yes," she said confidently. "I'm adamant."

3. Unfortunate Meetings

As I stumbled into the GP's surgery I didn't want to see anyone, definitely not Marcus and not even my doctor to be honest. I had flu and wanted to be in bed, not spreading my germs around the town. That I had flu was pretty obvious; half my work colleagues had already been absent from work with it and I had every one of the classic symptoms. The treatment was, I already knew, to rest, keep warm and take plenty of fluids. Clearly I'd have been better off at home in bed and in staggering reach of a kettle. My boss didn't see it that way. No doctor's certificate for absences over five days meant no pay. No pay meant no flat, no cosy bed and nowhere to plug in my kettle.

I hate to think how many people I infected on the bus, but I'd been in no state to drive and couldn't possibly have walked. Still my cough, sweaty skin, constant sneezing, and ever increasing collection of damp tissues kept people at a reasonable distance.

You'll have gathered that, as well as feeling awful, I didn't look my best. So naturally Marcus was sat there waiting. Not for me obviously, but to see his own doctor. You'll have come across people with a bit of a sore throat who claim to have flu, I'm sure. Or seen the love interest in a romantic comedy supposedly suffering, but looking as flawless as usual? I've always maintained that if the patient looks as though anyone at all, including their mother, could possibly want to kiss them then they don't have flu.

Marcus, I was fairly sure, did have flu. For the first time

ever he was looking less than perfectly kissable. Even so, I went and sat next to him. For one thing, I had no need to worry about us passing on germs. Also, as every single time we'd met had been a disaster, why worry about him witnessing my impression of a red nosed zombie?

"Hi, Marcus." At least I avoided the ridiculousness of asking an obviously sick person, encountered at the doctor's, how he was.

"Hi, Sal. You got it too?"

I nodded. Not exactly a scintillating conversation, but it could have been worse. Often it had been. Well, nearly always. Marcus is the best friend of my best friend's husband. I met him at Aleesha and Drake's engagement party. I wish I'd gone on my own, but I'm always socially awkward and, let's face it, an idiot at times. I'd given my overly possessive boyfriend one last chance. When Marcus had introduced himself as the prospective best man, to me the chief bridesmaid, Mr Jealousy had been at the bar. Marcus didn't chat me up or anything, all his conversation was about our mutual friends.

"If you have any funny stories about when they were first dating, or Aleesha has any embarrassing secrets you'd like made public in the best man's speech, let me know."

We were exchanging phone numbers so I could do that, and he was saying he looked forward to seeing me at the wedding, when my date returned.

Talking to Marcus by phone the next day had been no trouble at all. Well, no trouble once I'd got past apologising again for my date yelling at Marcus to get his hands off me and inviting him to step outside and, "sort this out like real men."

I next bumped into Marcus at the wedding practise. Or

rather I bumped my car into his as he was leaving the church car park. I was probably going too fast to make the turn even if his car hadn't been there but the shock of the collision didn't bring out the best in me. Because of him, the timing had been brought forward and I'd had to rush from work to get there just half an hour late.

I'd started to say so, or yell so, when he said, "Can we exchange insurance details by phone? I'm in a hurry?"

"What?!"

"And could you move your car, please, so that I can get out?"

I did, then stormed into the church demanding to know what his problem was.

"No problem. He's just in a real hurry or I'm sure he'd have stayed to talk to you," Drake said.

"Something more important than his best friend's wedding practise?"

"He's got an interview for a fabulous new job," Aleesha explained. "It involves a lot of travelling so he has to prove he's reliable at getting to places on time. We said not to bother with this, but he didn't want to let us down."

"Ah." I could only hope the damage I'd caused his car was as superficial as it had looked and wouldn't delay him.

I didn't have a jealous boyfriend to take to the wedding, as I'd finally dumped the bully, but I was still an idiot, so I asked someone from work to come with me. That bloke got the idea that me collecting him and driving him to the function and him eating and drinking all day for free meant he'd be entitled to come back to mine and replicate the activities which would no doubt be going on in the honeymoon suite. Once I'd made it clear that wasn't the case, he tried the same thing with another, far more willing, bridesmaid.

Marcus and I had both decided to call it a day fairly early on, so we came across the pair of them in action, not just in the car park, but over the bonnet of Marcus's car. A car which, by then sported an un-dented front wing in a different colour to the rest of the bodywork. Oh and this happened right after I'd asked after the job interview and been told that not only didn't he get it, but our collision had caused a leak in the radiator which led to him breaking down and having to spend a night in Manchester. The extra time off meant he was lucky to still have his other job. I wasn't surprised he didn't wave as he drove away.

We'd met again on a couple of other occasions, but thankfully the doctor's receptionist called my name before I had a chance to recall Aleesha's dinner party where I'd suffered an allergic reaction to the pre dinner nibbles another guest brought, and… Actually that's probably all the real disasters. Our other meetings have just been awkward and embarrassing.

My doctor gave me the expected advice about resting, keeping warm and taking lots of fluids. She also gave me a mini lecture about going out in such a state, pointing out it was irresponsible in terms of both my own health and that of everyone I met, but at least she wrote out the certificate which had made my reckless behaviour necessary.

Marcus was sitting by the door as I left.

"You've not been seen yet?" I asked.

"Yeah. I have."

I supposed just walking as far as his doctor's office and back had tired him. It hadn't done much for me either.

"How you getting home?" he asked.

I explained about the bus and learned he lived just opposite where I needed to catch it, thankfully very close to the surgery. We did our best to help each other stagger there.

"When's the next one?" he asked.

The tiny numbers on the timetable swirled before my eyes. Then they did the same to Marcus. No one else was waiting, which suggested it wouldn't be any time soon.

"Cup of tea while you wait?" he offered.

Rest, tea, Marcus. I'm not so much of an idiot that I refused. There was a quilt on his sofa, so I pulled it round me.

Marcus placed two mugs and a bottle of whisky on the coffee table. "Want some of this in it?"

I accepted and sipped the steaming drink. Whether it was our tiredness, the warmth of the quilt or the whisky I don't know, but the next thing I remember is fumbling for my phone and realising I wasn't at home and wasn't alone.

"Sal, shall I let myself in?" Aleesha's voice asked, the moment I answered.

"What? Where?"

I learned she'd gone round to my place after work to see how I was and of course couldn't get a reply. She has a key for emergencies, but despite what you might think of me, hadn't ever needed to use it.

I explained that I was with Marcus. Well perhaps explained isn't the right word because I wasn't exactly sure myself why I was curled up in his arms as he continued to snore. I rather liked the warm safe feeling though and the snoring was pretty quiet considering how bunged up his sinuses must be.

Marcus was awake by the time Aleesha arrived. She hadn't come empty handed. One bag was stuffed with things like my frog slippers complete with lolling tongue, Barbie pyjamas, prettiest underwear and toothbrush. Another bag contained the fresh items from my fridge.

"I always knew you two would get together," she said. "Might have known you'd make him ill when you did, Sal!"

We did try to explain, but only got as far as saying we'd met in the doctor's that morning.

"Have you eaten?" she demanded.

Aleesha cooked us an omelette, poured a pint of orange juice into each of us and insisted we went to bed.

I ate, drank and said I should go.

"Stay," Marcus said. "It's warm, we can sleep."

Put like that it sounded so reasonable.

Sleeping was about all we did for the first twenty-four hours, waking only to use the bathroom and eat the food Aleesha provided. By the next day we talked a bit and I slept on the sofabed again the second night. We decided I'd stay; it was easier for Aleesha to do her very welcome Florence Nightingale act and although we both felt terrible we didn't think we'd prefer to be alone with our misery.

We discovered we liked Scrabble, a surprise to both of us as we'd not played since we were kids and had been sceptical when Aleesha delivered the board along with further food supplies. We were equally bad at it to start with, but as our health improved our scores went up. I think he beat me a few more times than I beat him, but we were still fairly well matched. I had the chance to earn a treble word score, but only if I used a very rude word (and don't forget F and K are worth four and five points respectively).

He grinned as I laid down the tiles. "Sorry, Sal I still don't have the strength for that!" He didn't look shocked, at least not until he added up my total score.

It wasn't just a liking for Scrabble we had in common. We enjoyed the same films, music and food we discovered as we began to recover. We liked each other, enjoyed being together. Although very pleased we were soon well enough to fend for ourselves, I was sorry to leave Marcus's flat. I know he felt the same way.

My guilt and sympathy for Aleesha and Drake when they both went down with flu was heartfelt, but I couldn't help being just a tiny bit pleased it would mean sharing nursing duties with Marcus. That was until we met at their house in our lunch break. Somehow, in less than a minute, I managed to spill fruit juice down the front of his trousers. As he changed into a pair of Drake's, I decided to help out by putting on a wash. Marcus returned, wearing trousers a good three inches too short, to ask what the clanking noise was.

His mobile phone was responsible, as it turned out. Well, how was I to know that he'd anticipated some kind of disaster would result from our meeting, so had removed his jacket and draped it over the laundry basket for safety?

Marcus must either have liked living dangerously, or liked me as much as I liked him, because even after Aleesha and Drake were well, he wanted to continue seeing me. Not every meeting was a complete disaster and to be fair not every problem was my fault. Honestly, that stray cat I persuaded him to take in was so skinny no one could have anticipated it giving birth just as Marcus had been about to take me to dinner.

All the little snags, awkward moments and complete

catastrophes had one thing in common; they occurred as, or right after, we met up each time.

"When you stayed with me while we had flu, nothing went wrong," Marcus said.

"True. We weren't well when we met, but we got better together."

"And when we went to Wales for the weekend everything was fine."

"Yes." Well it had been once we'd got there which was later than planned as I'd tried to meet him at the wrong train station.

"So we should live together. They'd be no more meetings, so no more problems."

And that's what we did. It's been great so far. Last week though Marcus had to go away for work. I have to meet him at the airport in half an hour. It's just started to snow. Wish me luck?

4. I Must Protest!

"… and obviously I'll put something in the City Herald," my granddaughter Elly said.

She's just started there as a trainee reporter although how the people she interviews get a word in, I couldn't tell you.

Elly had come round to help with the planning of our Golden Wedding party. I know it's a cliché, but I can hardly believe my gorgeous George and I have been married almost fifty years. Some mornings I reach over and touch him, just to prove to myself it hasn't all been some marvellous dream.

"We could go really retro and have the same food as you had at your reception," Elly suggested. "At least I can look up what would have been available. I don't expect you to remember."

"That's right, better check Sir Walter Raleigh had discovered potatoes by then!"

Elly started to protest, but I cut her off with a laugh. "Prawn cocktail to start. Then roast crown of lamb, new potatoes, baby carrots, minted peas and cauliflower cheese. Afterwards there was Black Forest Gateau, coffee and wedding cake. We drank Mateus rose wine and thought we were terribly sophisticated."

She'd taken notes as I described the food. "We could do all that, if you'd like?"

"The lamb would be tricky. Goulash might be better and it would be easy enough to do something similar for the vegetarians, with fancy mushrooms instead of the meat."

"Brilliant. That's the food all sorted. Now for the decorations. Did you have a colour theme, or anything?"

I fetched the album. In several of the photos guests held up placards. In one we were shown leaving the church under a tunnel of 'protest' signs which actually carried good wishes.

"What's that about, Gran?" Elly asked.

"It's because so many of our friends knew the story of how your grandfather and I got together."

"Go on then, spill!" Elly demanded.

"When I was twenty-two I worked in a factory which made biscuits."

"I knew that, you… sorry, I didn't mean to interrupt."

"There was this chap there I really liked. He was handsome, bit of a rebel."

"Grandad was?"

"Do you want to hear this?"

She pretended to look contrite. "Yes."

"Then don't interrupt."

"Sorry, Gran."

"And I was pretty, slim and shy – and you'd better not be thinking of doubting that!"

"You're still pretty, Gran." She smiled sweetly.

"Hmmm. Anyway I heard him say he was going on a protest march. Before you ask, yes we had them then. I made sure I overheard him when he arranged to meet some others who were taking part. I just happened to bump into them, after I'd spent the morning making myself look beautiful. It worked and he invited me to join them."

"What were you protesting about?"

"Testing cosmetics on animals. I heard some horrible things."

"It is terrible and it's shocking it still goes on now."

"I quite agree with you, but some of what I heard was nothing to do with putting shampoo into rabbit's eyes. Instead they were talking about smashing open the laboratories and inflicting the same treatment on people who worked for the companies concerned. I didn't want any part of that."

"Don't blame you."

"I let myself fall away from that group and joined some women who seemed less violent. They were in favour of peaceful protest all right, but to me they appeared even more obsessive. None used any products which could conceivably have been tested on animals."

"That's good, isn't it?" Elly asked.

"If a woman chooses not to put on lipstick that's her business, but avoiding soap and toothpaste seemed extreme."

"Ah. Yes."

"I started thinking there must be a more reasonable approach. Shouldn't there be a way people could know how the cosmetics and toiletries they used were produced and so avoid those which involved animal testing?"

"There is Gran. The leaping bunny logo."

"Now there is, but not back then."

"So you and Grandad helped make that happen?"

"Who is telling this story?"

"Sorry, Gran."

"I was lost in lots of ways; in my thoughts and in the crowd. I'd lost sight of my rebel boy and lost interest in him by then. Partly because of his apparent intent to break the law and hurt people. Perhaps even more because at work he'd ignored me and only noticed me that day because of my short skirt, tight sweater and false eyelashes. He had no real interest in me."

"He does now. Grandad adores you!"

A warning look silenced her.

"I lagged further behind until another young man said I looked as disillusioned as he felt. I explained that everyone seemed so extreme. He said the same. He was a reporter and very much against cruelty to animals, but feared that by expressing the opinions of some marchers he'd not do much to help."

"Oh! That was… sorry, go on."

"He interviewed me and very tactfully helped out with leading questions as gaps in my knowledge became evident. Over the next few weeks he did a series of features about the protests and my search to follow fashions and look good without causing suffering to test animals. We weren't the only ones by any means, but yes, I do think your grandad and I played a tiny part in making it much easier to buy cruelty-free products."

"What you did was great, but I am a little bit disappointed you and Grandad weren't really a couple of gorgeous, dangerous rebels."

Then she turned the page of the album to see George in his leathers on his motorbike, with me in a tiny skirt and long, long boots riding pillion. There was a placard, strapped precariously to the machine, declaring us 'Just Married'.

"OK, you were kinda groovy."

I handed Elly another album, full of George's newspaper articles on the subjects we care about. Illustrating each was a photo of the pair of us, on marches, handing a petition into No 10, even chained to the fence at the Greenham Common peace camp.

Finally Elly was quiet. Speechless with admiration, I like to think.

5. Run Aground

As usual for a Sunday, or any other day come to that, Lynn woke up alone in the bed. Andrew would be downstairs making tea. He'd bring her up a cup, tell her what the weather was like and then say he was off bird watching.

"Would you like to come?" he always asked for form's sake.

"Not today, I have things to do," she always replied. Then, when he was gone, she'd try to make the housework fill the morning. They had a roast on Sundays but, apart from the meal choice, every day was much the same, rather dull, routine since they'd retired.

As expected, she heard Andrew climb the stairs. Unusually though he crept quietly into the room and put the tea on her bedside table without a word.

"It's OK, I'm awake," she told him.

"Oh good. I didn't want to disturb you, but it didn't seem right going without saying anything."

"Going?" For a horrible moment she thought he meant he was leaving her. She wanted a change, but definitely not that.

"I've seen on the internet that a ship's run aground at Southampton Water. Apparently they're going to try moving it at high tide. I thought I'd go and take a look."

"Oh, those poor people." How terrible to be setting off on a cruise, or catching the ferry over to the Isle of Wight and for that to happen. It certainly put her boredom into

29

perspective.

"I think the crew are all safe," Andrew said.

"And the passengers?"

"There aren't any. It's one of those car carrier things."

"Do they know what happened?"

"Not yet, but the local news will have updates, I'm sure. It'll be on the radio too, so I'll listen in."

"Switch it on for me, will you?" The radio alarm they no longer needed was on his side of the bed.

It wasn't until he'd done as she requested Lynne noticed the time; quite a bit earlier than he usually went out. She hadn't realised he got up so early. She didn't know he looked at the internet when he got up either, and wouldn't have guessed he'd be interested enough in a stricken ship to miss out on bird watching. It seemed she hardly knew him at all.

"Will you be back at the usual time for lunch?"

"Yes, I doubt anything much will happen for a while, I just thought I'd take a look. It's a good birding spot. Or…"

"What?"

"I could just take a look and come back, I mean we could, if you like?"

"Oh, I…"

"It'll only take a couple of hours at the most and this kind of thing doesn't happen very often."

"That's true."

It sounded as though he hoped she'd come, and there was more than two hours to go before she'd need to put the meat in the oven. It would be something to talk about when she spoke to the children too. They always asked what she'd been doing and the answer was usually nothing.

"Yes, all right," Lynn said, surprising herself as much as her husband.

"It'll be cold," he warned her. "Put on lots of layers." He fetched her coat, hat and gloves as she got dressed and gulped down the tea.

On the drive round they kept the radio on low so they could catch any news updates and Andrew told her what he'd found out from the internet about the ship, its cargo and intended destination.

"The sea between here and the Isle of Wight is very shallow in places. To get out safely, ships have to follow special channels which are kept dredged. For some reason this ship went slightly off course and is now stuck on a sandbank."

The local news came on the radio and Lynn turned up the volume. Very little information was given, less even than Andrew had already told her. The reason for the grounding was, apparently 'unclear'.

A pop song came on and Lynn adjusted the volume. "Could it have just taken a wrong turning?"

"I doubt it was quite as simple as that. If the captain isn't familiar with the port then he has to have a pilot on board. They know the route well and help and advise."

"So what could have happened? Not pirates or terrorists surely?" She'd wanted some excitement in her life, but not that kind.

"Unlikely," Andrew reassured her. "If there'd been the slightest hint of that it'd have been all over the internet. Maybe the stormy weather we've been having moved the sandbank, or the ship's steering failed."

Lynn was surprised he was so knowledgeable, but then he spent a lot of time on the coast looking at birds and talking to those who shared his hobby, and others who'd come to photograph ships. She supposed he'd picked up some information.

They joined a slow moving queue for the last part of the journey and were lucky to find a parking space.

"It's never this busy, not even in the summer holidays. The ship must be drawing a bit of a crowd."

Andrew was right. There were people everywhere, carrying cameras and binoculars and all heading in the same direction. Dozens and dozens of them. Lynn and Andrew joined the group on the beach.

Even though she'd come to see a stranded ship, Lynn got quite a shock. It was right over on its side, the edge of the deck practically in the water. How frightening it must have been when that happened. How fortunate that whatever had gone wrong occurred so close to land so help was quickly available.

Now though the drama was over. The crew were safe. The ship, stuck fast and going nowhere. She knew the feeling.

The crowd who'd gathered were saying it was the pilot's fault or the captain's. There was talk of people being fired or sued. Lynne was pleased her first thought, when Andrew had told her of the grounding, had been for the safety of those on board, not who to blame. Andrew too had thought it might be an accident rather than jumping to the conclusion of negligence or worse.

"Why blame anyone? Couldn't it have been an accident?" Lynn spoke almost in defiance of those around them.

"It could have been, probably was, but ultimately it's

always the captain's fault; at least technically."

Was that true of her, Lynn wondered. Yes, she was captain of her own ship, wasn't she? Maybe she was stuck in a rut because she hadn't steered correctly… really she hadn't been steering at all for some time, just drifting. She never looked ahead, or even out to the side. Never had, there didn't use to be time. Raising the children, housework and she and Andrew having fulfilling, demanding jobs left them little time for themselves or each other. Now they'd retired they were where she'd thought they wanted to be. They had time to lie in bed, to sit and watch the birds, do whatever they wanted, but they weren't really anywhere, certainly not on any chart she might have plotted.

It wasn't deliberate. She'd not actually steered them into trouble. Neither had Andrew. An accident then? The steering, rather than being mishandled, had simply broken? No one's fault… except that it hadn't been maintained had it, their marriage? Not recently. Andrew seemed to have given up and she'd never really made an effort.

There was a brief flurry of excitement when a camera crew turned up to film the stricken ship and watching crowd. After that people began to drift away. It seemed nothing much would happen until high tide, over an hour away.

"What will happen then, do you know?" Lynn asked.

"Maybe they can pull it off the sandbank with tugs. I'm not sure though. That might cause more damage, especially to the cargo which must have moved. Without the water holding it afloat the tugs might not shift it and it'll have to be salvaged where it is."

"Salvaged?"

"A team would make it safe, pump out the fuel and that

sort of thing. They'd take off what cargo they could, then cut the ship into pieces."

That sounded drastic. "Is there no other way?" she asked.

"Before we came out I read the hope was she'd float free with the rising tide. It's possible I suppose, but I can't really see it happening."

Lynn, looking at the exposed keel of the ship and seeing the high tide mark on the beach, had to agree with him. They weren't as stricken as this ship though, she and Andrew. They didn't need tugs, or for their marriage to be cut to pieces. They just needed a little water under them to get them moving.

"Shall I take you home then?" Andrew asked. "Do you have things to do?"

"No, not today. What would you have done now, if I hadn't come with you?" Lynn asked.

"Gone and looked at the birds for a while, then come back and see if anything was happening with the ship and if it was, stay and watch until it was time to come home for lunch."

"We could do that together, if you like."

"I would like that." He gave her the smile she'd almost forgotten.

"Of course, if I'm not there to cook it, there won't be a roast but it wouldn't hurt to have something else for a change."

Andrew led her to a quieter spot and pointed out the elegant white egrets, the smartly patterned oystercatchers and aptly named yellowlegs. Lynn quite enjoyed borrowing his binoculars and searching them out. It wasn't something she'd want to do all day every day, but it made a nice change from Sudoko and daytime TV. More importantly she saw Andrew was really interested, it wasn't just an excuse to get away from her for a few hours most days.

Actually he'd always been interested. He'd taught the children to identify the various visitors to the bird table and he still put out seed each morning. And before that, when they were dating and first married they'd gone together on bird spotting walks and he'd talked about how nice it would be to have the money to go further afield, maybe spend weekends in Wales or the Lake District. There had been things Lynn had wanted to see too, places she'd have liked to visit. Then had come the children and there'd been no time for any of it.

"Andrew, you don't have to go without your roast dinner," she said.

"You want to go home?"

"Actually, I thought we could go to a pub somewhere nearby for our lunch, that's if the ship isn't moving by then. Then we could come back here afterwards, make a day of it."

He broke into a broad grin. "Good idea."

"And maybe other times we could go out a bit further away. There's that swan place you once said you'd like to go to and I'd love to visit where they filmed Downton Abbey and if we made a weekend of it we could go down to Kent where some of Call the Midwife was made. They probably have different birds there…"

Andrew chuckled. "Bluebirds over the White Cliffs of Dover?"

She knew he was teasing her; he'd explained once that the Bluebirds were an American species which never visited British shores.

"That sounds like a wild goose chase to me," she said.

"Wild geese are considerably easier to find. I'll show you some this afternoon. Hundreds and hundreds of them." He looked happy, really happy.

"That's an impressive salvage team!"

"Sorry, love. I'm not with you."

"I'll explain it when we have time, but for now let's see how that ship's doing, then find somewhere for lunch, go look for the geese and after tea maybe we can start making plans for next week."

"Come on then," he reached out and took her gloved hand in his.

Unlike the ship, they'd taken a turn at the last minute and avoided going aground. Now they could plot a course and sail out of the shallows. Who knew where they'd end up?

6. Blind Date

Lindsay shrank under the taunts that she was mousy in looks and personality. "Four eyes and no friends," other girls called. Or, "Lindsay Goring is so boring."

Knowing it was true didn't stop it hurting.

"But it's not," her brother Daniel, back from deployment, said. "You're sweet and quite pretty in your way." He suggested a plan to silence her tormentors and so allow her confidence to grow.

At Saturday's disco the other girls watched the stranger dance. Lindsay's quick glance showed her Daniel's tall, broad shouldered silhouette.

"Stand aside girls, he's all mine," Lindsay bravely declared.

They laughed at her words. Jeered as she stood and strode towards him. Shut up as she tapped him on the shoulder and waited for him to turn and face her. Gasped when she kissed him.

"Nice introduction," the stranger said.

Perhaps she'd been wrong to discard her glasses. Perhaps not.

7. Just Being Practical

For the first time ever, Margaret felt nervous about going to see Richard. Yesterday he'd seemed uncomfortable; as though he felt he should say something, but couldn't quite bring himself to do it. It had never been like that between them and they'd known each other for almost thirty years.

At first it was just as neighbours. Richard lived a couple of houses down the road. He and his wife had taken in parcels for Margaret and her husband. They'd exchanged a few words if they walked by the other's house when they were in the garden or putting out the bin. Friendly, but not actually friends.

Then, when Richard lost his wife and Margaret lost her husband within a couple of months, they'd teamed up. Not so much to help each other through it; they both had friends and family for that. It was for the practical stuff.

"My attempts to iron my clothes do nothing to improve their appearance," he'd said one day when he looked particularly untidy.

"I hate climbing ladders," Margaret said to explain the lack of a working lightbulb in her hallway.

Neither of them thought it worth cooking a proper Sunday dinner just for one person. So she'd go round and iron his shirts while he roasted a chicken, or he changed her lightbulbs or climbed into the loft to make sure the water tank was properly lagged as she cooked for him. They shared 'buy one get one free' offers at the supermarket, taking it in turns to drive there.

It was nice to have someone to chat to during the day. Someone she could just mention things to or share a cup of tea with when she was bored with her own company. It was good too, to feel useful. Margaret's family were very kind but they always wanted to look after her. They didn't chat really either. They asked how she was and had the big important conversations, such whether she would stay on in the house and if she could cope alone. And they kept trying to cheer her up. She didn't want that. Of course she didn't want to be miserable, but neither did she want to be jollied along.

She and Richard never talked, they just chatted. It was pleasant, undemanding company. They didn't share dreams and plans, just arrangements for the next day or the weekend.

One day when her daughters called in, she told them she'd cut a 'two for one' voucher from the paper and was visiting a stately home with Richard. Soon after, Margaret overheard them saying it looked as though she'd found someone to ease the pressure on them and take their dad's place.

"But I haven't! I loved your father and miss him terribly. How could you think I've forgotten already?"

"We didn't mean that, Mum. It's just that we're pleased you're not moping around and have Richard now. We like him."

"I do not 'have Richard', whatever you mean by that. We're just neighbours who help each other out now and then!"

"OK, sorry," her youngest said.

"That's fine," added her eldest. "And if you two ever become more than that, well, that'd be fine too."

Margaret didn't discuss the matter with the girls again,

but she did talk to Richard about it. "My kids seem to have got the wrong end of the stick about our relationship. If they have, other people probably have too."

"Who cares what anyone else thinks?" Richard had asked.

That was a fair point. Those close to her knew the truth, now she'd explained. If others wished to gossip and put two and two together to make five, that was their business. What Richard and she thought was important, so Margaret made sure she was extra practical after that.

They'd got into the habit of watching TV together in the evenings if one of them happened to mention they were going to watch something the other planned to see. Margaret didn't want to stop that, she enjoyed the company and it was gratifying to have a witness when she got questions right on Mastermind or University Challenge, but really it was no more practical than watching it alone. Margaret rectified that by combining her viewing with a useful task. She sewed on buttons or darned socks as they watched. Obviously she could have taken his clothes to her house to do that, but it was more practical to do it at Richard's place.

Once she was looking for ways to be useful, she found plenty. She took down Richard's curtains, washed and replaced them. Of course he had to do the actual hanging, involving the stepladders as it did.

"If you want to wash yours I'd be happy to take them down and put them back up," he told her.

"Yes please."

They had lunch together and then watched a film on TV as the curtains whirled round in the washer and dried on the line.

Richard noticed her tap dripped occasionally. "I could

replace that for you," he offered.

She accepted and they drove into town to buy a replacement. "Might as well make the most of being here," he said. "Let's have a coffee and cake."

It cost almost as much to park the car near the library for one hour as it did for the whole morning, so it seemed practical to visit the museum or art gallery whenever they exchanged their books. They had several other similarly sensible arrangements and Margaret thought their relationship would continue in the same way indefinitely.

She'd thought that right up until yesterday, when Richard had been trying to talk to her. No good kidding herself, he definitely had and he'd not been happy about whatever it was. Could he be ill? Not just a cold, but something serious? Margaret truly hoped not. She didn't want to lose him. As that thought came so did another. It was nothing to do with his willingness to climb ladders, the convenience of sharing supermarket bargains or only having a roasting pan to wash on alternate Sundays. She liked him. Liked him a lot and not just as a friendly neighbour.

Richard didn't seem ill, Margaret tried to reassure herself. Of course you couldn't tell. If Richard really was she should make the most of whatever time they had left together. That was practical in a way, wasn't it? She wasn't sure if he felt the same way about her, but as she'd only just realised how she felt herself that was probably no guide.

Margaret decided she'd drop a subtle hint and see how it went. Of course if something came of that and she lost him she'd be hurt again. But she would anyway, why not have some happiness first if they could?

She took a few deep breaths and went to see him. Unusually for him, he fussed about inviting her to sit and offering tea. Normally he'd have just assumed that if he made it she'd drink it. He was definitely as nervous as Margaret felt herself.

She followed him into the kitchen, hoping she'd spot something useful she could do and which she could concentrate on as she tried to work up the nerve to hint at her feelings for him.

Richard stepped back from switching on the kettle and bumped into her.

"For goodness sake just sit down, will you?" he said.

He'd never snapped at her before. Not even just after they were both bereaved and were tetchy and irritable with everyone's well meant words of sympathy.

"I was just going to…"

"Well don't," Richard said. "I don't want you acting like an unpaid housekeeper. You don't have to do all the things you do for me."

"Oh." Perhaps he'd seen her attempts to provide practical help as interference? Maybe she really had been interfering?

Now she knew she cared about him, Margaret saw she'd been making excuses to spend ever more time with him. Just as she had, when her children had treated her as helpless, Richard must be resenting the way she seemed to think he couldn't cope. She tried to explain.

"No, it's not that at all. I want you to see that I care about you, Margaret. I care about you as a person and not just someone who does useful things for me."

"Oh."

"You mean a great deal to me," Richard said.

"Oh, I… that is…"

"Maybe I shouldn't have said anything but I thought you

must realise something was going on. I keep trying to find things I can do at your place or you can do here so I can spend more time with you. It was getting silly. I know you like to be practical and washing all our curtains every month is hardly that."

"I suppose not, no."

"It would actually be more sensible to leave them up and go out somewhere fun for the day, wouldn't it?"

"Yes, it would… as friends, you mean?" She didn't think he did mean that, or not just that, but she'd already seen it was easy to misinterpret their relationship. Friends wasn't exactly what she wanted, but it would be better than nothing.

"I was hoping for more than that, but friends would be a lot better than nothing," Richard said.

"I was thinking," that wasn't actually true as Margaret was saying this on the spur of the moment. "Running two houses between us is hardly practical, is it? We could sell one and share the money between our children and live together." Her words even surprised Margaret, but once she said them it seemed to her to be a good idea.

Richard looked thoughtful for a moment. She couldn't read his expression, but there didn't seem to be any alarm in it. "We could and you're right it would be practical." The kettle boiled and he switched it off. "Getting married wouldn't. We could spend some of that money on fancy clothes and food and inviting everyone we know to a big party. I'd like that, but it wouldn't be practical at all."

"I'd like that too and perhaps it might be practical," Margaret said.

"I don't see how."

"Neither do I, but we might discover something."

Richard pulled her close and kissed her. It wasn't unpleasant, not at all, but it would take some getting used to. Judging by how quickly he turned away and fiddled with the pack of teabags, even though there was already one in each mug, Richard felt awkward too.

"Or we could do it anyway, just because we want to?" Richard mumbled.

"We could," Margaret agreed.

"So that's a yes?"

"Yes. Oh! I've just remembered, champagne is half price this week. It makes sense to have something to celebrate if we're going to buy a bottle."

Richard grinned. "You're right, that makes our engagement very practical!"

He kissed her again.

It was even better the second time. Yes, that was definitely going to take a lot of getting used to. Margaret, very practically, kissed him back, just to get that important process started.

8. Sweets For The Sweet

Doreen stared at the beautifully wrapped, heart shaped box which lay on her doormat. Valentine's day was the right date for such a thing to arrive, but this wasn't the right address.

There was a card attached, in the same deep pink as the gauzy bow. That wasn't much help. It wasn't addressed to anyone and the message read, 'something almost as sweet as you, from your Valentine'. That could be for anyone. Well, not Doreen. It was 60 years or more too late for her to receive such things. When she'd been a girl her father wrote her funny verses, later her husband always bought lovely bouquets. Now both men were just happy memories. Today would be a good time to get out her scrap book of mementos.

First though, she had to work out who the chocolates belonged to. Maybe her old friend, Lancelot, could help? She knew he'd be happy to try. He was like that. It was a great comfort to have him living nearby again after so long abroad.

She felt a little shy, ringing him today of all days, but a mystery like this was just his sort of thing. Plus there was a chance he'd seen something.

"Morning, Lancelot. I was wondering if you could pop round? I have a problem to solve."

"Be right there."

"Have you eaten breakfast?"

"Not yet, but that can wait."

She had bacon and sausages sizzling in a pan by the time he'd crossed the road.

"Smells good," Lancelot said as she ushered him into the kitchen.

"A good meal always helps me think," Doreen said. "Would you like tomatoes and mushrooms too?"

"Oh rather. Thank you, Doreen. This is most kind of you."

He was equally enthusiastic about the suggestion of eggs and beans. "Now, tell me about this problem."

She showed him the box. "Did you see this being delivered?"

"I wasn't looking out the window at the time, but even if I had been, it wouldn't seem right to tell you who brought the chocolates. Presumably the gentleman concerned wishes to remain anonymous."

Doreen giggled. "I didn't think they were for me! They must be for one of my neighbours' girls, Pamela or Sue."

"It seems far more likely they're for you. Why else would they be put through your letterbox?"

"All the houses in the terrace look very alike. I expect the young man simply put it through the wrong door," Doreen explained.

"I suppose such a thing could happen. How do you hope to discover the intended recipient?"

Doreen was delighted Lancelot hadn't jumped to a conclusion about that. Most people would probably assume pretty, blonde and bubbly Sue at number eight was most likely. She was amusing and popular, but 'sweet' wasn't the word Doreen would use to describe her.

Pamela at number twelve, with her mousey looks appeared less likely to inspire tokens of love, but was an exceptionally sweet child. She regularly called on Doreen, especially in bad weather, to ask if she could fetch her anything from the shops. Doreen could just imagine how her usually pale cheeks would flush and her eyes sparkle if she were to receive a Valentine's present.

"You're absolutely sure this is for one of them?" Lancelot asked.

"As sure as I can be. Both girls have mothers and I sincerely hope their husbands still give them gifts for Valentine's, but they wouldn't have made a mistake over the address."

"True, true. I don't know the girls as well as you. Do they have gentlemen callers?"

Doreen smiled. Lancelot really did seem as gallant as the Knight he was named for.

"Both have something of the sort. To be honest, I don't want the chocolates to be Sue's. They'd make her all the more besotted with the latest boyfriend."

"You don't approve?"

"In my opinion, Frank's a bad lot. He often arrives late, or not at all, sometimes says unkind things to her and seems very controlling."

"I see."

Doreen brushed her hand over the box. The cream paper felt silky to the touch and was embossed with a gorgeous design of white and palest pink roses. "This doesn't seem the sort of gift Frank would choose."

Lancelot placed his hand over Doreen's. "I agree," he said.

"Pamela's male visitors apparently play chess, or discuss strategies for the school's debating team. They don't take her out anywhere. It's probably never occurred to them to do so. Sorry, that doesn't help us. If we get it wrong one girl will be unnecessarily disappointed."

"What will happen to the girl who gets the chocolates, if they weren't really for her?"

"She'll think she has a secret admirer. One year, before I met Gerald, I got a card. I never discovered who sent it, but I was still very pleased. Getting these might make the world of difference to Pamela's confidence."

"Then there's our answer," Lancelot said.

"But if Frank has been romantic and generous, it's only right that Sue should know."

"I'll go into town and get another box." Lancelot was back very quickly with an identical gift. "The shop in the High Street offers a wrapping service. Just as well, I'd never manage anything as fancy as this."

Lancelot asked for a sheet of paper to practice the handwriting, then copied the original message onto the second card using his left hand. Doreen, who couldn't tell one box from the other, acted as lookout while Lancelot delivered them.

"Thank you so much." She kissed him on the cheek. "Happy Valentine's Day," she whispered then went back inside.

Doreen fetched her scrapbook from the trunk in the spare room, but hadn't opened it before there was a knock at the door.

"Doreen, look at this!" squealed Pamela.

"Do you know who sent them?" she asked before Pamela

could ask something similar, forcing Doreen to lie.

"No." She sounded wistful.

"Do you know who'd you'd like to have sent them?"

"I wish it was Peter. He's just lovely."

"Have I seen him?"

Pamela's description was rose-tinted, but just accurate enough for Doreen to deduce which boy she meant.

"Oh yes, he does seem pleasant."

Pamela agreed; at length.

"What should I do about the chocolates?" she eventually asked.

"I should eat them, they look delicious."

"They are. Oh sorry, would you like one?" She offered Doreen the box.

"No love, they're all for you."

"But what should I do? Do I thank Peter? Maybe it wasn't him?"

"I'm no expert on these things, but I suggest letting him know that if they were from him then you're pleased, but you're not quite sure who sent them."

"Good idea." Pamela left soon after.

Doreen made herself a cup of tea and opened her scrapbook. She'd not found what she was looking for before she heard shouting from next door. She'd gone out to see what was wrong before realising it was Frank yelling at Sue, and stayed in case the young man did more than raise his voice.

"I told you, they're not from me so you're to throw them out," he commanded.

"I will not. You didn't send me anything so I don't see

why I shouldn't enjoy these."

"I'm not having you encouraging some other bloke."

"I haven't been. There's a lot of things you don't want me doing aren't there? You don't like me seeing my friends or being able to rely on you. I never know if you're going to turn up."

"Treat 'em mean, keep 'em keen," Frank taunted.

"I've had enough of you being mean, you're dumped." As she turned away from him, clutching the chocolates, she gave Doreen a grin. Sue would be fine.

Doreen went back inside and continued looking through her scrapbook. There it was – her one and only anonymous Valentine's card. Her thoughts were again interrupted, this time by the doorbell.

"Doreen, look!" Pamela brandished another box of chocolates. It wasn't so neatly wrapped as the others and didn't look nearly as expensive, but that didn't matter at all. Peter had bought them.

"When I told him about the others he rushed out and got me these. He said he didn't want me to be anyone else's Valentine."

The last few words were almost lost under the clatter of the letterbox.

Another heart shaped box of chocolates dropped onto the doormat. The message on the card was exactly the same as before; 'something almost as sweet as you, from your Valentine'.

"I don't understand," Pamela said.

"Neither do I, love. Don't worry though, you know who gave you these." She tapped the box from Peter.

"That's true. I don't suppose I'll ever worry about

anything ever again."

Doreen smiled at the girl's optimism and hoped it would stay with her a long time.

Immediately Pamela left, Doreen compared the handwriting on the gift card with that on her old Valentine. They matched. She found the sheet of paper she'd given Lancelot to practise writing left handed and discovered he'd written, 'Doreen, it's taken me far too long to ask you this, but will you come out to dinner with me? Your Lancelot.'

Doreen tucked the note into her scrapbook, then phoned to accept.

9. Bounce For Joy

Through the trees, Nadine glimpsed someone approaching. She shortened the dog lead, ready to turn around if, rather than the man she expected to meet, it was someone who might reveal her secret. A moment later Christian and his black Labrador were in view.

Bounce gave a bark of recognition and wagged his tail furiously.

"Go on then." Nadine unclipped his lead.

Bounce, true to his name, bounded up the woodland path towards Shadow and leapt about in an energetic game. They stopped briefly for the canine greeting of mutual sniffing, then resumed racing round in circles.

Nadine held her breath as Bounce hurtled at speed towards a tree, but it was OK; he changed direction at the last moment. She winced as he approached a muddy puddle, knowing what would happen there. Sure enough, he charged straight through, covering himself, Shadow and Christian in smelly mud.

"Sorry!" Nadine called.

"My fault for getting so close. I haven't got used to the change in him."

"Nor me," Nadine said. Just a few months ago, Bounce was timid around people and other dogs. Now he was generally less nervous and clearly enjoyed the company of Shadow and Christian. That's why Nadine often met up with them both. It was good for Bounce to socialise and he got more exercise chasing Shadow than he would simply from walking with her.

Christian was good company, but it was for Bounce's sake she'd given him her phone number and typed his into her mobile two months previously. It was for Bounce's sake that whenever possible, she timed their walks to coincide with Christian taking Shadow out. She hadn't mentioned Christian to her husband James, but that wasn't because she was doing anything wrong.

"How about walking over to The Monument today?" Christian suggested.

"I'm not sure…"

"Running up the hill a few times might just wear this pair out," Christian coaxed.

That was true, but it was a big risk. The Monument was a popular spot. Lots of people, with and without dogs, walked there. The chances of meeting someone who knew Nadine and James was fairly high. Unlike meandering woodland paths, where it was hard to recognise people until you got close, and easy to take an alternative route if you didn't want to meet them, Monument Hill was open grassland. If someone saw her and told James, he'd feel betrayed.

She hadn't lied to her husband, but she'd certainly misled him by letting him believe she needed time by herself for an hour or so each day. What choice did she have but to keep on doing it? Stopping these walks would break her heart.

"How about a stroll down to the ford?" Nadine said. "They could splash about and wash off the worst of the mud, if you have time for that?"

"I have."

As they walked side by side, Nadine began to feel guilty.

She'd told herself she hadn't wanted to go to The Monument because she didn't want to hurt James, and that was true… But was staying out longer than usual a better option? He might call to see where she was, or ask where she'd been.

"Christian, I'm sorry, but I'm going home."

"Right now?"

"Yes. I have to tell James the truth."

Nadine and Bounce set off at a brisk pace. Even so, she was likely to lose her nerve before getting home. She slowed, called her husband and tried to explain.

"I'll come and meet you."

As soon as James arrived he crouched down and fondled Bounce's ears. "Who's this and what's going on?" he asked.

"This is Bounce. I'm a volunteer walker at the rescue kennels and I've fallen in love."

"I can see why; he's a sweetie."

"I know I agreed we wouldn't have another dog after Rufus, but I never promised to keep away from them entirely. Please don't be angry."

"Oh, Nadine, I'm not angry. I only said we shouldn't have another because I didn't want you to ever again to be so hurt as you were when Rufus died."

"You can't stop that happening. If we adopt Bounce, of course I'll be devastated for a while when we lose him, but if we don't, I'll be miserable all the time."

"We'd best get him back to the kennels." James took Bounce's lead. "Come on, boy. Sooner we start the paperwork, the sooner we can take you home."

10. Unromantic Valentine

When an enormous bouquet was delivered to the office it caused huge excitement. Everyone was asking 'who's it for?' or wondering who sent it. Of course no one even considered it might be for Alison, especially not Alison herself. It wasn't her birthday nor the kind of flamboyant gesture her husband would make.

It would be the same on Valentine's Day she knew. Many of the other women would get cards, chocolates and flowers. One year there was even a man hired to serenade a particularly pretty blonde. Then Alison would be expected to listen to everyone's plans for the evening; dinner out somewhere, maybe the theatre or the promise of a weekend away. She was happy for them of course. It was just hard sometimes to really show it.

There was never anything like that for Alison. Bill didn't do that kind of romance. He'd probably make her breakfast in bed; a cup of tea and a slice of toast. No card, just a silly little note hidden somewhere for her to find during the day. Often it was too cheeky to show the girls at work even if she wanted to face them with a second-hand envelope or whatever scrap of paper Bill managed to find. He generally offered to take care of supper and got them fish and chips, plus a bottle of whatever wine was on special offer. This would be eaten in the light of a couple of candles stuck on a saucer. Afterwards they watched a romantic comedy then had an early night… though they never actually went to sleep earlier than usual.

She shouldn't complain. Over twenty-five mostly happy years they'd had. He was a good husband and she knew he loved her. She also knew he hated the commercialism of Christmas and Valentine's and she had to admit that he had a point. But oh, wouldn't it be nice if one of the pretty bouquets brought in was for her. Or even just a brightly coloured envelope bearing a soppy card.

Another thing Bill didn't do was subtle hints. If she wanted a lovely romantic gesture as a Valentine's surprise, she was going to have to spell it out.

Alison phoned her sister that evening, making sure to leave the door open and speak loudly so Bill heard every word. She rather warmed to her theme and moaned more than she really meant, but also made it very clear what she wanted.

On Valentine's morning Bill brought her a glass of Buck's Fizz and a bagel topped with smoked salmon. Alison forced herself to eat and drink the lot even though a piece of buttered toast was usually the most she could manage in the mornings. She remembered last year Bill cut a slice into a heart shape. To be honest she'd preferred that. Still he wasn't to know, was he?

At work she told the others about her luxury breakfast and agreed when they all said how thoughtful it was of him. The day's post included a huge pink envelope addressed to Alison. The picture on the card was suitably soppy as was the printed verse inside… but it didn't sound like the sort of thing her Bill would say. Never mind, the girls thought it was nice.

Then a massive bouquet of flowers arrived for her. That was more like it! Really lovely they were. Too big to go on her desk though so she left them in a sink in the toilets.

Almost everyone who went in came out wanting to know whose they were and once they knew, told Alison, 'Your hubby obviously really loves you.'

He did she knew. But then she already had known.

The flowers made progress down the street difficult and Alison missed her usual bus. By the time she got home she was feeling nearly as battered and bedraggled as they were starting to look. The idea of curling up on the sofa with a mug of tea while Bill popped out to get their fish supper was very appealing. She made sure to thank Bill profusely though for the card and flowers.

"Glad you like them. Now go and get ready, I'm taking you out for dinner."

"Lovely," she managed to say.

The restaurant was suitably decorated with heart shaped balloons and red roses. Candles glowed on every table. So many tables and all but one was occupied. They carefully followed the waiter to it and squeezed into the seats. The person to her left was closer to her than Bill. If Alison leant back she'd bang heads with the woman behind her and there was only nobody on her right because that was the door to the toilets. It was so noisy that any conversation, let alone murmuring sweet nothings, was almost impossible.

There was a set menu including several dishes Alison liked, though none of her particular favourites and oh, the price! Wine prices were even higher. As she ate and drank she couldn't help wondering how much the holiday fund would have been topped up if it hadn't been for this meal and those flowers.

By the time they got home it was already past the time they normally went to bed and Alison was exhausted from having to pretend she was having a wonderful time. She still had to put away her nice dress and remove her make up. The whole thing had been a disaster. Bill must have hated it though he didn't let it show. The worst part was knowing she only had herself to blame and had to find a tactful way of ensuring Bill didn't repeat it every year from then on.

The next morning Bill woke her with a cup of tea and a slice of toast.

"Oh thanks, love. I didn't hear my alarm go off."

"No, you must have forgotten to set it last night. Don't worry though, I've put your lunch ready for you."

"Oh thank you. Bill, I do love you, you know that don't you?"

"Of course I do, silly."

When she fumbled in her bag for her bus pass she found one of Bill's silly notes attached to it. Once in her seat she read, 'I love you every day, not just on February 14th. Sorry I'm not the most romantic of blokes. I hope you know how much you mean to me - everything. x x x '

Aaaw!

She discovered another note when she unpacked her sandwiches. She giggled out loud as she read what he planned to do that night to make up for them going straight to sleep the night before. The girls looked enquiringly at her but she didn't explain. This was between her and Bill, not something to impress her colleagues... which now she thought about it was the real reason she'd wanted a card and flowers sent into work.

At home that evening Bill said, "You go and have a nice bath and put your pjs on and I'll go out and rent us a film and pick up something to eat."

They ate fish and chips from trays on the sofa and washed

it down with cheap wine. They giggled through the cheesy film, then went early to bed.

That weekend Alison had another, impossible for Bill not to overhear, telephone call with her sister.

"Bill only went and did every one of the things I said I'd like for Valentines'! … Yes, I know I'm so lucky… Funny thing is I've realised there's only one thing I really want on that day; my lovely hubby."

11. Coconut Shy

Lorna carried the tray into the office. "There you go, tea just as everyone likes it." She grinned in anticipation of their by now traditional response.

"You're so good to us," one of her colleagues said.

"Not just good to us, good at everything!" another added.

"Totally talented!" said a third.

Lorna placed the tray on her desk. "Ha! Flatterers. But go on then, you can each have some of my homemade apricot flapjack."

"Did I mention I'm in awe of your talents?"

"Not quick enough to get two pieces you didn't." Lorna picked up her mug. "Now, what did I miss while I was slaving over a hot kettle?"

"Young Ashleigh here asked how we met our husbands. I told her a friend introduced me to mine, but nearly everyone else met theirs through work."

"Which is good news," another colleague added. "As she has her eye on that Colin in despatch. You know the one I mean."

Lorna did. "Good looking lad. If I were twenty years younger…"

"Forty would be more like it!"

"Cheeky, but true. Anyway I'm not looking for a husband. Tell the truth, I'm still quite fond of the one I've got."

"How did you meet him, Lorna?" Ashleigh asked.

"I won him at the village fete, but if you're trying to use our experiences to catch your own man, don't try that one. It was a disaster and very nearly a tragedy!"

Of course that meant everyone wanted to know all the details.

"Although I'd hardly even dated, my friend Sue was engaged. As I didn't want to stay single forever I asked her advice. Sue said I put potential boyfriends off because I'm so good at everything." She paused to give her audience time for their usual joke.

"Yes, Lorna. You're very clever."

"Totally talented!"

"There's nothing you can't do!"

"True, but don't go on so," Lorna said. "Anyway, according to Sue, a man likes to feel he's the strong capable one, at least some of the time. She knew her Malcolm liked her, but it wasn't until he fixed the puncture on her bike that they talked for long enough that she could drop hints about wanting to see something at the pictures. By the time her tyre was inflated again, and she was really grateful, he got the courage to ask."

"I don't fancy cycling to work," Ashleigh said. "The roads round here are so busy."

"Don't blame you, love, and I knew nothing like that would work for me either. If I'd got a puncture I'd have had the bike upside down and wheel spanners in action before a knight in shining Spandex had spotted what was happening. Besides I only had problems like that when I was on my own."

"Yeah, your friend was lucky for it to happen at just the right moment," Ashleigh said.

"That's what I thought, but she confessed to having brought a carpet tack out with her and riding round until she found Malcolm on his own."

"Oh!" Ashleigh looked thoughtful.

"I realised I'd been relying on just happening to bump into the right man, who'd instantly fall in love with me – and that the chances of that happening were very slim." Lorna sipped her tea. "I knew all the cool boys would be at the village fete. Not for the fete itself, they weren't exactly hip even back then, but some of the lads liked to park their motorbikes and pose on the green where it was held, and I was pretty sure they wouldn't be able to resist an extra large audience."

"You fancied a biker?" Ashleigh asked.

"I did. Remind me to show you some photos of me back then and you won't be quite so surprised. Anyway, my plan seemed to be working. The boy I liked detached himself from the group, paid his sixpence or whatever the entrance fee was, and went around the stalls in the same order as me. When I got to the coconut shy, I resisted the urge to make an accurate throw. Instead I chucked the ball wildly, in the hope he'd come to my rescue and win it for me."

"Did it work?"

"No, Ashleigh love, it didn't. As I was aiming the wrong way, I shouldn't have thrown it hard enough to knock the nut from the metal ring… It hit another lad on the head. Poor George was stunned, so although he realised I was the efficient woman who cleaned and dressed his wound, he didn't suss I'd caused it. He was grateful for me patching him up and we became friends, until the day I admitted what I'd done."

"Bet he was cross!"

"Nope. Until then George had found me a bit intimidating, on account of thinking I was really good at everything." She paused again.

"Which you are!"

"Totally talented."

"Yes, yes. Enough of that. Once he realised I was capable of messing up, he found the courage to ask me out."

"So Sue had been right?" Ashleigh asked.

"Oh… yes. I suppose so. Talking of being good at things, I'm afraid tea break has overrun a bit and we must get back to work."

The following day Lorna needed to query something with the despatch department and requested one of them come up to the office. Young Ashleigh was in the kitchen, making tea, when Colin arrived but returned to the office in a hurry. She accidentally stumbled over an out of place wastepaper bin – falling straight into Colin's arms! She was quite shaken, so he suggested she come and sit outside in the sunshine with him until she felt better.

"Looks like I'd better see to our tea," Lorna said, getting up and putting the bin back in its usual safe place. "What fool left it there?" she asked, hoping nobody had noticed who'd used it last.

"We don't know, Lorna. But can guess who gave young Ashleigh the idea to come racing in just when she did, apparently not see it and then fall so gracefully in that particular direction."

"I haven't a clue what you're talking about," Lorna declared. "Anyone fancy a slice of coconut cake? I'm really good at making that."

12. Bridge Of Oich

"Who's an oik?" Nikki asked, once the adverts came on.

"No one," John replied.

That was a matter of opinion, but she tactfully didn't say so. "Then what were you talking about?"

"I thought we could go to the Bridge of Oich this weekend," John suggested. "It's near the top end of the Caledonian Canal, so we could do both at the same time."

Nikki put her empty coffee mug down, with a touch of emphasis. "You said you'd take me out, but as usual it's all about what you want. I suppose you've found out Thomas Telford built the bridge and that's why you're interested now?"

"No it's not like that, love. You said you'd like to see it. It was when we went to Inverness to see Neptune's Staircase at the other end of the canal, remember?"

They'd not just seen it, but studied every inch, or so it had seemed to her. The details had faded from her memory, but she recalled being bored and then grumpy. "I remember we didn't have time for the one thing I wanted to do." Unlikely as it sounded, that really had been a visit to the Bridge of Oich.

"You were right, it was too far to go in one day, so we missed it. Sorry about that, I should have realised. This time I thought we could book into a hotel for a couple of nights and have time for everything we both want to do. You could have a proper browse round Eastgate shopping centre too."

"Oh. Yes, that sounds all right." She remembered her shopping trip to Inverness retail park on the way to Telford's flight of locks was the reason it was getting dark by the time John had finished looking round and taking photos. That's why she'd not seen the bridge, and also why he'd not seen the other end of the canal, which naturally he'd have liked to. She was starting to feel just a little bit guilty for moaning at him.

Nikki collected their mugs and took them into the kitchen to wash.

On the drive over to Inverness she said, "Let's see the canal first. That way you'll get plenty of time there." Plus that would get the boring part out the way and she could then enjoy the rest of the weekend.

"Are you sure, love? We're passing quite close to the shopping place; it would be no trouble to call in."

"You've been looking forward to seeing that canal for ages. I won't make you put it off any longer."

"Thanks, love." He took one hand off the wheel to squeeze her hand. "You're good to put up with my interests. I know engineering isn't really your thing."

She felt a little guilty about that too; shopping most definitely wasn't his thing but he trailed around, trying to look interested, and carrying all her bags. Besides, he could be forgiven for thinking she would have some interest in all those bridges and canals and things, given her background.

Nikki tried to summon up some enthusiasm in the canal as John took his pictures and made notes. There were a few pots of flowers, which brightened the banks, and the nearby houses had pretty gardens. The weather was nice and made the water sparkle. She supposed the canal with all those locks was quite ingenious and watching five boats get brought in and lowered down to the next level was sort of interesting. At least it was the first time. The novelty had worn off long before the boats reached the final lock.

Although bored herself, she could see John was enjoying the experience. She didn't want to drag him away before he was ready, nor make him feel bad that she wasn't having much fun, so told him she was going for a walk.

"Would you like me to come with you?"

It was sweet of him to ask. He nearly always did put her first, but instead of appreciating that, she got irritable the few times that wasn't the case. She must try to stop that. "No, that's all right. I'll just have a look round and see what there is. If there's anything interesting, I'll let you know."

"OK, love. See you later then."

Nikki found quite a nice gift shop where she picked up a few little things for the grandchildren. Apart from that, a kind of farm place with rare animals which she didn't fancy at all, a few pubs and restaurants, and a small supermarket, there really wasn't anything to see. Oh well, it had killed some time and she'd spotted Oich Road so knew where they'd have to go to see the bridge; the one engineering project she was keen to see. Walking back to join her husband she checked her watch; she'd not been gone even as long as she'd guessed and John wouldn't be ready to leave yet. Perhaps she'd look at the menus on offer in the places overlooking the canal. If she chose one of those for lunch he could spend longer gazing at the water gates and levers and she'd be sitting down with a glass of wine while he did.

The first pub she tried seemed perfectly suitable, but she checked all the others too. That's how she ended up in the exhibition; she just walked down the path and through the door without realising what it was. Once inside she didn't like to admit her mistake, so spent a few minutes reading the display boards, which unsurprisingly were mostly about Thomas Telford. The man had obviously been very clever and did amazing things for the time. She could understand some of John's obsession with him. Nikki browsed through the merchandise on offer. Much of it was the same as she'd already seen, but the postcards were different and quite cheap. She selected an aerial view of the canal and one which showed a painting done when it first opened. John was sure to be interested in those. Should she buy him a book too? There was a television in their hotel room so she was hoping not to miss her soaps. If John had something new to read then she wouldn't feel at all guilty for watching them. Trouble was she had no idea if he already had the ones on offer. He probably did.

Their lunch was rather nice and, as she'd guessed, John was pleased with the view. What she'd not anticipated was that more boats would arrive while they were eating and she'd have to trail after him to watch them all go through in the other direction. Her earlier intention not to get grumpy gradually deserted her. Hours they'd been there by the time he'd seen enough. Two at least, and getting on for three hours if you included lunch. Then to cap it all he drove off in completely the wrong direction.

"Haven't you forgotten something?" she demanded.

"I don't think so, love."

"The Bridge of Oich?"

"That's where we're going now."

"It's back the other way."

"I don't think so."

"I do! Of course you made sure you knew exactly how to get to the canal, but when it comes to what I was interested in, it doesn't matter if we find it or not!"

"I'm sorry, love. I really thought this was the way. I'll turn round and you can direct me."

Nikki did her best, but it seemed her husband wasn't the only one who didn't care whether people saw the bridge or not. It wasn't signposted. They drove very slowly down Oich Road looking for clues until they stopped at the end. They repeated the process in the opposite direction with no luck.

"Park the car and we'll walk down," Nikki said.

The moment he stopped she jumped out and headed back to Oich Road. She heard him call her, but fearing she'd just snap or complain if she said anything, she ignored him. She strode on, walking parallel to the river Oich and looking through the trees for a glimpse of the bridge. The one place where she might have got a decent view was locked up. Nikki wasn't going to be beaten. John had taken dozens of pictures that morning, she wasn't leaving without at least one photo of the bridge. John was absolutely no help. While she looked for the bridge he just stayed by the locked gate reading a sign and calling out, "I really don't think this is the right place, love."

"Of course it is," she called back, as calmly as she could manage. "This is Oich road and that's Oich river and it goes into loch Oich and that's the only bridge over it except your precious Telford's swing bridge!" She continued down a treacherously slippery path, inching through the plants growing along the river bank now and then, hoping for a good view.

There it was! Well, what was left of it which wasn't

much. It looked like a few old trestle tables on stilts. Her view was obscured by trees. To get a clear picture she'd need to be out in the water. Luckily a small boat was tied up alongside. Trying to row out would be crazy, neither she nor John had any experience and anyway there weren't any oars. The pointy end was resting on the bank though. If she got in and went down the other end she'd be a good bit further out and should get her picture.

Reaching the boat wasn't difficult. Once she moved towards it gravity sent her down the bank. Nikki reached for the edge of the boat and performed what felt like a somersault, but was probably just an undignified flop. Either way she was in the boat and it was swaying in the most alarming manner. The bottom wasn't exactly dry either. Still she shuffled along a kind of bench seat until she was at the far end. Leaning out as far as she dared, she took her picture. She was shuffling back again before John even noticed what she was doing.

Her grumpiness was no aid to getting out of the boat. If the dratted thing had stayed where it was when she got in, then getting out and up the bank would still have been trickier than getting in – but it had moved. The rope was still securely attached to a tree, but instead of lying slack it was now pulled taut and there was a considerable expanse of water between boat and bank. It probably wasn't further than she could have jumped if she'd started from somewhere stable and would have been landing somewhere flat. She was sure it was further than she could manage from the edge of a wobbly boat onto a steep and slippery bank.

"What are you doing, love?" John asked when he reached her.

"I've decided to join the Marines, what does it look like?"

Sensibly he didn't answer and instead hauled on the wet rope until the boat once again touched the bank.

"Did you get your picture, or shall I come in and try?"

Wisely, given that the water level inside the boat was rising, she didn't get into an argument about being just as capable as he was of taking a picture.

"No thank you. I've got one and I'm not sure the boat can take both of us. I'm beginning to think it was abandoned for a good reason."

"Give us your hand then and I'll help you out."

She first handed over her camera and then, with John's help, scrambled out. Once they were back onto the road they both had muddy shoes, splashes of river water on their legs and an all over smell of wet dog. She felt foolish for behaving so rashly, and having to be rescued. To make matters worse, John stopped at the end of the swing bridge and looked down the river. From there Nikki had a clear view of the wooden bridge. That's what he'd been trying to tell her right from when she left the car.

"Perhaps you could take a picture for me?" she said, as a kind of apology.

He did, then they walked back to the car. When John drove off again it was in the direction he'd been going when she pointed out his mistake. It wasn't the way they'd come, so presumably not the way to the shopping centre he said they'd passed close too. She kept quiet though; she'd been grumpy with him for days, just because he'd been so engrossed in a new book about Telford that he failed to immediately compliment her new perm, and she'd almost got herself drowned because of it. For once she'd give him the benefit of the doubt. Maybe he was heading for their hotel. A shower and cup of tea actually sounded more appealing than several floors of retail outlets right then.

They'd not been travelling long when John pulled into a tree fringed car park.

"What are we…? Oh." She'd just spotted a sign directing them to the Bridge of Oich. "That's ridiculous. There shouldn't be two!"

To add to her discomfort John apologised for taking her to the wrong one the first time.

"No, John it wasn't your fault. It was mine. Sorry."

"Easy mistake. It was by Oich Road and over Oich river, which I suppose does make it an Oich bridge, just not the Bridge of Oich."

"I suppose so," she agreed.

"Come on, let's have a look."

The bridge, when she saw it, did at least look like a proper bridge, not a tied together pile of wood like the other one. It was metal, painted white and strong looking. When she said so, John laughed and said, "Better than that boat! You go stand on it and I'll take your picture."

She could hardly complain when he took more pictures of the bridge and read the signs about it.

"Seen enough?" he asked after they'd been there longer than she felt strictly necessary.

"I have, thank you."

As they walked back to the car, John asked, "Why did you want to see it anyway? Not quite your sort of thing I wouldn't have thought."

"Remember when you first met Dad?"

"I didn't make much of an impression, did I?"

"No!" She laughed at the memory. "Dad didn't really

believe in your interest in historical civil engineering and thought you were just sucking up."

"Actually I was a bit to start with, but once I took an interest I got really interested, if you see what I mean."

She did. She'd always avoided getting interested herself for fear she'd became as absorbed as her father who spent all his spare time researching and writing books on the subject. As a child she'd felt neglected in favour of boring old construction projects and as John's interest had grown it seemed history was repeating itself.

"He claimed you wouldn't know the Bridge of Oich from a pile of driftwood," Nikki said.

"He was right!"

"He wasn't though was he? You knew. It was me who didn't."

"Well…"

"Can we keep that bit quiet? Can you imagine what he'd say about his daughter making such a mistake?"

"Nothing, he'd be speechless with shock."

She grinned at him. Dad did tend to act as though he thought she must be fascinated by the subject and as he tended to lecture rather than discuss, hadn't realised she didn't have much of a clue.

"Anyway," Nikki said, "I didn't believe there was such a place as Oich and thought he was calling you an oik. We had a, er, disagreement over it."

"You rowed with your dad over me?"

"Yes. You probably have that to thank, or blame, for us being together. I wasn't sure about you at first but I couldn't dump you then on principle. As I got to know you I found I liked you. Well, you know that." Did he though? She'd almost forgotten herself and she certainly hadn't shown it lately.

He put his arm round her shoulders. "It was different for me. I knew straight away you were the girl for me. I loved you the minute I saw you. And still do, of course."

There was no of course about it. She was lucky to have him. Lucky with her father too. He'd not seemed an ideal parent at times during her teenage years but she appreciated him now and knew he wanted her to be happy. Recently he'd reminded her of the Oich/oik incident and she'd wanted to see the bridge for herself. Had Dad been giving her a nudge back towards John? Probably. Once he'd seen her boyfriend's interest, in Nikki at least, was genuine and that she cared for him, he'd encouraged the relationship.

Nikki realised John had said something and as so often of late she'd not been paying attention.

"Sorry, what did you say?

"I thought we could go into Inverness for some shopping now if you like?"

"Shopping? Yes. Maybe a shower first might be a good idea though?"

"It would and maybe a cup of tea?"

"Absolutely."

As they drew near the Caledonian Canal once again, Nikki asked him to stop. "There's something I want to buy."

"Here?"

"Maybe." She took him back to the small exhibition she'd accidentally visited earlier. After giving him a few minutes to look round, she asked him if he already had the books on display.

"Yes, love. I have. Is that what you wanted to buy? A

book for me?"

"Yes. Not to worry though. I'm sure they'll have bookshops in Inverness."

"I'm sure they will."

"Actually, why don't you go and look at them while I do the shopping I want to do? We'd both be happier that way, wouldn't we?"

"We would," John said. "Just one thing though, let's be very sure which bookshop we're meeting in. I don't want to be in trouble if one of us goes to the wrong one."

"Dad was right about you. You are an oik!"

"Yeah, but you love me."

"Yeah, I do. I really do."

13. Flying From The Truth

Angie lays out their stuff on the bed; swim-wear, shorts and T-shirts, her black dress that never creases. Patrick's shorts have a slightly larger waistband and her swimsuit is less revealing, but otherwise the clothes are just as they've always been. It'll be their usual two weeks on a sunny beach, so she packs suntan lotion. This year things are a little different, so there's a lot more lotion. Everyone knows how dangerous it is to get burned.

It's not just the packing that's changed. They're not quite the same people they were on their last holiday, two years ago. They've never really needed a holiday before, but they do now. Last year they didn't take one. Last year Patrick's mother was dying of cancer. This year they've watched her slowly waste away in St Mary's Hospital. They've buried her and sold her house and tried to continue their own lives. Booking a last minute deal to the Dominican Republic had seemed such a good idea.

"Patrick," Angie calls, "do you think we need that mosquito repellent thing?"

If Patrick goes to look for it, he'll see the letter. She'll be forced to tell him the truth. Jim, dear Jim, has been begging her to tell him. She left one of his notes in the drawer where they keep all those things that might come in useful, but never do. Things like the plug-in mosquito repeller that never worked properly.

A flash of colour outside the window catches her attention. A child is flying a red and yellow kite.

"Patrick," she calls. "Don't bother. The travel agent said we won't need it."

Jim will say she's a coward. Jim will be right, but it's not just that. She will tell Patrick, but later. Let him enjoy a few days of the holiday first. Let her try to do the same. They'll both be stronger then, able to deal with it.

The Caribbean is as beautiful as promised in the brochure. They stroll past beach sellers offering paintings and mobiles and carvings. Colour and shapes in endless variety.

"Special offer for pretty lady," one skinny seller calls out to Angie.

She knows he's speaking to her, but feels ugly. Not on the outside, she looks good on the outside. For the last few months she's taken great care of her appearance. Jim said she looks better now than when he first saw her. Patrick hasn't said anything.

"Special offer for American," the seller tries Patrick.

"We're English," he replies.

"Double special offer for English," the boy says.

Patrick's mouth laughs, but there's no smile in his eyes. It's like something has died, not just his mother, but something inside him. Maybe she's left it too late to tell him the truth. Maybe Jim was right.

"It's his life, his marriage too. If it's not going on much longer, he has a right to know, to prepare himself," he'd said when she'd first admitted her feelings to him.

"I don't want to hurt him until I have to," she always said.

"He's probably already realised something is wrong. You've lost weight, you're away a lot, you don't always want him to touch you," Jim said just last month.

"You understand me so well."

"So does he. You should tell him."

She'd said she would. Promised she would. She hasn't packed the mosquito repeller, but has brought the letter from Jim that repeated his plea to tell Patrick everything. When they get back to their hotel room and change for dinner, she slips the note into the book she's reading. The envelope is longer than the pages, so she turns down the end. The book looks as innocent as she and hides the same secret.

"They're giving Spanish lessons this evening," Patrick says after they've both pushed the food around their plates. "I thought I'd go, would you like to come?"

"No, I'm a bit tired. I think I'll just sit and read my book. Will you get it for me?"

She finishes her drink while she waits and orders another. The ice melts.

Patrick doesn't say anything, just hands her the book. The envelope is still there, but the end is no longer folded over. There are shadows under Patrick's eyes and the rims are red.

He doesn't say anything though. Why doesn't he say anything?

"Another drink?" he offers.

Patrick goes to the bar. He comes back. He seems to have forgotten the Spanish class.

He looks tired and defeated, but he's looked that way for a long time. She doesn't know if he looks worse, doesn't know why he hasn't mentioned the letter. Maybe he didn't read it? The note was just a single sheet in the smooth white envelope. Perhaps he thought it was empty and simply smoothed out the fold she'd made.

She'll tell him tomorrow.

"Shall we buy a kite today?" she asks.

"Aren't we past all that?" Patrick says.

She doesn't answer. There is nothing to say. Flying a kite was their thing. Every holiday they bought a kite and tried to fly it. They'd started on their very first holiday together. They'd not had much money to go on trips, but had enough for an old, faded, kite they spotted in a second hand shop. Every year since, they'd bought a kite, the brightest one they could find. They flew it during the holiday, then left it behind with local children.

Instead of buying a kite, they take a coach trip into the mountains. The lush scenery is gorgeous and the guide informative, but it isn't as much fun as it would have been larking about on the beach with a kite soaring into the perfect blue sky before crashing to the golden sand. She can't tell him on a coach full of people.

"Will you walk with me on the beach?" she asks when they get back to the hotel.

They walk on the beach, deserted for the evening. Slowly, they pass stalls now empty of colourful bric-a-brac. There's nothing there but the words she must say.

"You saw the letter from Jim?"

If she hadn't been looking for it, she'd have missed his nod.

"Why didn't you say anything?"

"It wasn't a surprise, Angie," he whispers.

"You didn't say anything before."

"I didn't want it to be true."

She can't face the truth or talk about it, why should he be different?

"Why him? He was best man at our wedding, for goodness sake!"

"Because he understands."

"I thought I understood you."

"You do, but I didn't want to hurt you, especially after your mum …"

"So you had an affair with my best friend?"

"No, Patrick! No, no."

He doesn't seem to have heard. "He comes round when I'm working nights, you go out and don't tell me where, you've lost weight and bought new clothes."

"Jim was right. He said you'd know something was wrong and I should tell you."

"Are you leaving me?" He speaks so softly she almost doesn't hear. Maybe he doesn't want her to.

"No! Not if I can help it. Patrick, I'm not having an affair."

"What then?"

"I wanted to tell you when I first suspected. I couldn't… because of Mum, so… I went to the doctor."

"You're ill?"

She nods.

"I had to speak to someone and Jim was the first person I bumped into. Literally bumped into as I was crying. He said I should tell you, but…"

She must make Patrick understand. If she doesn't recover, he'll need a friend, need Jim.

"And then your mum came home. Home to die. I couldn't

tell you then and when she was with us, I tried to block out my own… problem."

"Cancer?" He doesn't say the word aloud, of course he doesn't. He mouths it as he sags onto the sand.

Angie drops down next to him and takes his hand in hers. She can't say the word either. She presses her cheek against his and feels his tears.

"I told myself I didn't tell you because I wanted to protect you, but that's not true. I was too scared to talk about it."

"Is there… can they?"

"The lump is small."

"A lump? So you couldn't let me touch you. Yes, I see."

"I'll have an operation next week. Then radiotherapy if I'm lucky, chemo if not. I have to go to St Mary's. I know it will be difficult for you to go back there, but will you take me?"

"Of course." He hugs her. "I'm sorry I didn't trust you."

"I'm sorry I gave you reason not to." She is, very sorry.

Patrick pulls her close as though to squeeze out the lies and unhappiness.

"Tomorrow, let's go and see if we can get a kite. I reckon that skinny guy with the dreadlocks will have one, don't you?" Patrick says.

She nods. Tomorrow they'll fly a kite and after that they'll face what comes. They'll face it together.

14. Shop 'til You Drop

"I said your obsession with shopping would be the death of you," Oscar said.

"I'm not dead," Rachel pointed out. It was true she'd had an accident, resulting in a broken left arm and dislocated right shoulder, but the arm was set in plaster, shoulder back in place and she was out of hospital.

"No, thank goodness, but you're in a bad way. Still at least you won't be shopping for a while."

She had to agree. "I'm not happy about that, but only because it's inconvenient. I'm not obsessed."

"Could have fooled me! You're out nearly all day every day at the shops and every evening you're online looking for the best deals."

"If you want the bargains you have to keep on top of things."

He wasn't being fair. Her purchases were household necessities; food, cleaning products and the like. The way he went on anyone would think she spent all her time buying shoes.

"Is saving a few pennies on tea really such a bargain if it takes all week to get the groceries?" he asked.

She used her free bus pass to travel to the different shops and supermarkets so couldn't see why Oscar made so much fuss. Her falling down the steps in the precinct was possibly made slightly worse by the fact that she'd had a heavy bag in each hand but it wasn't caused by Rachel making full use of the buy one get one free promotion on their favourite brand of soup.

"Make us a cuppa shall I?" he suggested.

"Yes please, love." She felt guilty then. He was doing everything for her and not making a fuss about that. It wasn't any fun not being able to wash or dress herself. A tear trickled down her cheek, soon followed by a torrent of them when she tried to wipe it away.

"Hey, what's wrong?" Oscar asked.

"Tried to wipe my own face," she said. "It hurts."

"I know love. Here, let me." He wiped her face, then held her tea so she could sip it. "Better?"

"Thank you." She sniffed.

"You're not are you?"

"What are we going to do? I can't do anything…"

"Not just now, no. It'll be OK though. You set up the internet order for our food shopping, remember? When there was that offer on."

She did remember. By shopping online she'd had everything delivered and got £5 off the bill.

"That offer is finished."

"Yes, but it means I can get all the basics without having to go out and leave you for too long. I'll order some ready meals. They won't be as good as your cooking, but I should be able to heat them up OK. I already know how to run round with the vacuum and wash up. If you tell me what to do I expect I'll manage the washing machine."

"You don't need me at all, do you? I'm useless. I thought I was doing the right thing, trying to save us a bit of money now I'm not earning, but I've messed that up…"

"Hey, is that what all the shopping is about? You feel useless?"

Rachel nodded. "I suppose."

"That's silly. You're supposed to be enjoying your retirement. We're supposed to be enjoying retirement. I see less of you now than I did when you were working."

It was true and searching out bargains was tiring. Occasionally if she'd got a really good deal on something she'd feel elated, but usually she was exhausted and slumped in front of the TV when she was home. They used to go out for meals and socialise but lately she'd not had the energy.

"I'm going to show you what you've been missing," Oscar said.

"No, Oscar. I'm sorry but I can't go for meals out or visit our friends if you'll have to feed me. I'll make time for that when I'm better I promise, but please wait until I can at least hold my own glass of wine."

"OK, but I'm not taking you shopping and I'm not having you sitting around home brooding."

He took her to the pictures. It was nice to sit back and relax when she wasn't too tired to concentrate on what she was watching.

When she felt a little stronger, they went for walks together and attended talks in the library and at the gardening club Oscar had joined when he'd retired. Oscar held the door for her and helped her on and off with her coat but he'd always done that so it didn't make her feel awkward.

Once she was fully recovered Rachel said it was time she returned to doing her share of the chores and that included the shopping. She set out after lunch armed with a small bag and her bus pass. She visited just the one supermarket. Even so it took her quite a while as everything had been moved round since her last visit and it took time to decide which items offered the best value. Rachel had no intention of proving she wasn't bargain obsessed by spending recklessly. It did make her see though that her previous ruthless money saving efforts had their own cost in wasted time.

Oscar opened the door for her before she'd had the chance to put down her bag and look for her key.

"I'll put this away, you go and get changed ready to go out to dinner," he said.

"That's a lovely idea, but what's the rush?"

"I remembered what you said about it paying to shop around. I looked online and discovered there's 20% off at the Red Lion if we arrive before seven. Oh and the pizza place does a similar deal, so I've booked us in there for next week. And, um for Sunday Lunch at The Swan. They do free desserts for pensioners on the last week of each month."

Rachel smiled to herself as she got changed. It seemed as though Oscar had developed a mini obsession of his own. Still, if eating out every week would make him happy she didn't mind going along with it. She didn't mind at all.

15. Boy Next Door

I didn't like my neighbour much. That was OK – he liked himself enough for the two of us. He knew enough for the two of us as well, or thought he did.

When I first moved in I was actually quite impressed. There was neither too much, nor too little of his dark, shiny hair. He was tallish and broad shouldered, but not intimidatingly large and muscular. His clothes were clean and tidy, his manner polite. Best of all was his smile.

"Hi," he said. "I'm Mark. Welcome to Bulldog Crescent." He had a pleasant voice. Deep, yet gentle.

"Hello, Mark. I'm Jenna. It's nice to meet you."

Before I could say another word he gave me the benefit of his superior knowledge on the neighbourhood – where to park if I wanted to shop in town, best place to get coffee, which roads got blocked during the school run etc etc. Yes, that seems nice and neighbourly and helpful and everything. No, it isn't his fault I knew already because my previous home was just a mile away. The point is, he didn't ask if this was information I wanted or needed.

No, it wasn't exactly that. Mark's attitude was very much that of making an effort to be charming to the new girl. Which still sounds fine, I know, but… He treated me as though I didn't belong, when a wish to belong was precisely why I was there. As I was growing up our family moved frequently, and lived in rented accommodation, because of Dad's work. It didn't bother him. I don't think Mum was keen, but she made the most of it, saying it was all great research for when they finally bought their own place.

My sister saw it as a great opportunity to make lots of new friends and constantly reinvent herself. "If no one knows anything about you, you can be anyone you want." She was always trying out new looks, new hobbies, new personalities almost.

Although I did try to be positive, I didn't want to keep having to start again with people who didn't know me. I wanted to fit in, share some history with those around me, even if they remembered my mistakes as well as my triumphs. Really I wanted my neighbours to know and like the real me. I didn't want to be an interesting new arrival, or someone passing through, I wanted to belong somewhere. Perhaps even to someone. The sort of relationships you know will end in a few months weren't the kind I wanted to begin.

I'd been delighted when Dad and Mum finally bought a permanent home in a picturesque market town. My sister moved to the city at the first opportunity, but when the time came for me to get my own place I only moved a mile away.

Most of my new neighbours were retired, friendly and chatty. They proved Bulldog Crescent was the kind of community to which I'd always wished to belong. Nearly every day someone would pop round to borrow something, offer homemade baked goodies or pass on snippets of news. Mark was the same… almost. Everyone else managed to arrive when I looked OK and had a moment to chat. He'd knock when I was dying my hair, exercising or on the phone.

The one day I was running a bit late for work, he asked me if I'd like him to put my recycling bin out. "They'll be collecting a day early, because of the bank holiday."

He couldn't have told me the previous evening, when incidentally I'd been wearing a dress I look rather good in, but more importantly would have meant I'd have had time to put it out myself, could he? He had to wait until I was the only one whose bin wasn't out on the road. The only only person who clearly didn't know how things were done on Bulldog Crescent.

"Yes, I know," I'd inaccurately informed him. "I don't have enough in it to be worth bothering." That wasn't accurate either.

It wasn't that I cared particularly about his opinion you understand, just that I wanted someone to feel that I belonged. To care whether or not I was staying put.

Guess which of my neighbours just happened to be passing, when I was shoving a big bag of recycling stuff into the boot of my car a few days later. In an attempt to get the paper, cardboard and milk cartons in before he saw, I managed to rip the flimsy sack open and spill the contents everywhere.

We both reached for the box which had contained a family sized Black Forest Gateau. As his hand clasped mine I felt a tingle… of annoyance. I wanted to explain I hadn't eaten it all myself, but had shared it with a couple of neighbours. Mentioning that might have seemed rude however, as he might feel I'd deliberately excluded him, rather than accidentally picked the one day he'd worked late. The two of us are never in synch, which reminds me…

Recently my sink got blocked and I'd crawled underneath and unscrewed the u-bend which released a jet of foul smelling gunk all over me. Mark tapped on my door just as I was about to remove my disgusting T-shirt. Honestly, if any other single man had kept coming round the way he did, I'd have thought they were interested in me as more than a neighbour, but with him it felt as though he were trying to catch me out.

"Plumbing trouble?" he correctly diagnosed, presumably from the smell. "Would you like me to take a look?"

Maybe I should have been grateful for his offer of help, but I wasn't. For one thing I'd already solved the problem. Until he'd arrived, I'd felt pleased with myself over that. His presence reminded me that none of my female neighbours would have done the job themselves. They'd have called in a nice, strong male neighbour; Mark.

The fact that, although he always looked good, he often saw me at my least attractive didn't bother me in the slightest. Why would it? It was the way he always made me feel like an outsider which irritated me. Clearly he considered me one. Three weeks ago I was about to go food shopping when I overheard him asking another neighbour if she'd like to contribute to a bouquet of flowers he was sending to someone, from all her friends on Bulldog Crescent. He didn't ask me.

I wasn't having that. In a short period of time I'd just about convinced the other residents I was one of them, but by excluding me from this, he'd undermine that.

"Mark," I called after him. "I'd like to put some money towards the flowers."

He looked surprised. "That's nice of you, Jenna. I'm sure Patricia will appreciate it." He said it as though he thought that highly unlikely.

No way was I going to admit not realising I had a neighbour of that name. Not to him. Besides, whoever she was, I couldn't imagine that knowing a new arrival had chipped in for her flowers would diminish her pleasure at receiving them. If it made Mark feel slightly less happy at handing them over then too bad.

I fumbled in my bag. Why can you never find your purse when you're in a hurry? And why when you need two or three pounds in cash, do you only ever have seven pence and a twenty pound note? "I hope she feels better soon," I said as I handed him the note.

"The flowers are for her hundredth birthday," he explained as he gave me change. "Patricia was ninety-eight when she moved away and we promised we wouldn't forget the occasion."

Oh, so she'd been gone at least a year before I arrived and Mark's surprise at my calling after him wasn't because I was dressed in clean clothes and my face free from smears. I didn't feel at my best though.

I felt a bit sick as he walked away. I don't mean uncomfortable that Mark always saw me looking awful or acting strangely, but that I felt like I was coming down with something. A colleague had been off work with a stomach bug, so I guessed I'd caught that. I stayed indoors, keeping myself warm, resting and drinking plenty of fluids over the weekend. Unfortunately that didn't stave off the bug.

Having got ill just as I'd been intending to restock the fridge and kitchen cupboards was unfortunate. So was knowing my condition was infectious. When my kind, elderly neighbours called I was forced to turn them away, without even opening my front door, for fear of passing it on.

Each time, I pushed open the letter box, croaked, "Please keep away," and crawled back into bed. Or the bathroom, but I'll spare you too many graphic details.

By the time I could have kept a meal down, I didn't have the strength to cook anything, nor any food left which could be consumed without going to that trouble. I'd not washed, or changed out of the same pair of pyjamas for days. My stomach and throat ached, my head was muzzy, my legs weak. From somewhere I could hear a dull thudding sound.

Looking back I realise I was dehydrated and my blood sugar levels seriously depleted due to hunger. Those things meant I lacked the sense to call a doctor or attempt to get help. All I wanted to do was sleep. A sustained pounding on the door wouldn't let me.

"Open up, Jenna!" Mark demanded. "I know you're in there and I'm not going away until I know you're OK."

I tried to shout. I don't know quite what I'd intended to say, but it didn't matter as my sore throat allowed only a muffled whimper. I tried to ignore him and sleep, but he really wasn't going anywhere.

In slow, exhausting stages, I staggered to my front door, opened it and fell into Mark's arms.

He nursed me himself, as he'd already been exposed to the germs. Everyone else on Bulldog Crescent joined together to help towards my recovery. They ran errands, cooked tempting little meals, left flowers, cards and good wishes.

By the time I was well, Mark had caught my bug. I went round to visit him several times a day, taking the gifts from our neighbours and doing all I could to keep him comfortable and encourage a swift recovery. He looked awful, with unwashed hair and stubbly face. He didn't have the strength to thank me properly, but that didn't matter. Thanks to Mark rallying the neighbours to help me, and then my doing the same on his behalf, I knew I'd become an accepted part of the little community. Mark had given me what I'd wanted for so long; to belong somewhere.

And to someone. Mark and I now have some history together. Not much, but we're building on it. We've seen each other when we've not been at our best. Neither of us intend to go anywhere anytime soon, except perhaps for one of us to move in with the other.

Like I said at the start I don't like my neighbour. No, my feelings are much stronger; I love him.

16. A Grand (Central) Romance

Robyn was entering Grand Central when her cell phone gave a burst of cheery music. She moved over to the wall, so busy commuters weren't inconvenienced as she answered.

"Hi, Robyn," her boss said. "Just heard your meeting has been put back an hour. Gives you time to grab yourself a coffee or something."

"I'll do that. Thanks."

She certainly would. Robyn usually did grab herself a coffee to go, on the way into work. Today she'd have time to sit and savour it. The drink wasn't the only thing she was pleased to have more time to enjoy.

Robyn loved Grand Central even when rushing to catch a train. She liked being surrounded by her fellow New Yorkers all going about their business, it gave a feeling of being part of something. With time on her hands she admired the impressive architecture and feeling of light and space. She stopped to gaze at the wonderful green ceiling, adorned with golden images of the heavens. It was nice to linger by the florist stall, inhaling the scent of carnations and stocks, and watching people buy gorgeous blooms for friends and loved ones.

Most of all Robyn loved Grand Central's food court – one stall in particular. It was there she'd been heading since she received the call. The coffee was excellent and the service exceptional. She knew Brandon, the handsome barista, would smile as though she'd made his day just by walking in, and pay her a compliment when he served her.

On cold days Brandon said the wind had put roses in Robyn's cheeks and joked he'd buy her flowers as soon as he got the nerve. He noticed when she'd had her hair done and pretended he wished he was taking her somewhere to show it off. Once when handing her a coffee to go he said, "Maybe you'll take me away one day?"

Much as she enjoyed this mild flirting, and wished he were serious, she knew it was just an act. No doubt something he did with any female customers he thought would appreciate his light-hearted banter.

His smile was even wider than usual, and caused his golden brown eyes to sparkle extra brightly. "I was thinking you weren't going to come today," Brandon told her. He said it as though that would be a genuine disappointment.

"Actually, I'm going to be here for longer than usual."

"Lucky me."

"And lucky me. A works meeting was delayed, so I'd like my coffee to drink in and a slice of that wonderful looking cheesecake, please."

"Should I be flattered you chose to spend your free time here?"

Robyn didn't know how to reply to that, so smiled and took a seat with a good view – of the counter where Brandon worked.

He brought over her drink and dessert. Thankfully he didn't say anything else of a flirtatious nature. Although Robyn had imagined many such conversations between them, in reality she wouldn't have known how to respond to anything beyond casual banter.

The coffee was as rich and aromatic as ever. The cheesecake was utterly delicious. The strawberry topping sweet yet tangy, a crumbly buttery base and the creamiest most indulgent filling. Perfect... just like the barista. Of course she watched him, and of course she noticed his competent hands, slim waist, neat dark hair and those heart melting eyes. For the first time Robyn also noticed how he behaved with other customers. He always smiled, was always polite, took the time to say something pleasant to everyone. But his smile didn't light up his face and make his eyes sparkle in quite the same way it did when he greeted her, and no matter how pretty the customer, those flirty compliments were missing.

If he didn't do it to everyone, then there was a reason he said those things to her. Was she reading too much into it, or had Brandon meant all he'd said? Just as Robyn was starting to believe that was true another coffee shop employee arrived. With barely a word to him, and not even a glance at Robyn, Brandon left.

She couldn't understand it. OK, she'd made a mistake in imagining he had feelings for her but, as he didn't know that, it wasn't the cause of him running off. Presumably it was just the end of his shift, but why hadn't he said goodbye or at least waved? That would have been polite and he was always polite.

She soon got her answer. Relief flooded Robyn as she realised he hadn't said goodbye, as he'd only left for a moment.

Her delight at his reappearance increased when he presented her with the most beautiful bunch of pink roses and said, "I told you I'd find the nerve one day."

17. Finding A Nice Man

"Muuum, I was wondering…" my daughter Carmel's tone was suspiciously casual.

"Yes, love?"

"Aunt Sheila said you've stayed single because of me. Is that true?"

"Partly, I suppose. But don't blame yourself. I'm sure if I'd met someone special you'd have accepted that."

"I'd like to think so. I definitely would like you to meet someone nice now. I worry about you sometimes."

"Are you saying you've stayed single because of me?" She's twenty and there's never been a serious boyfriend. It had never occurred to me I might be the reason.

"Partly, I suppose… Silly us! We should both find a nice man."

I was suspicious again. One for her or one for me? Having my sister matchmaking was bad enough. I didn't want my daughter joining in.

"Is it difficult for someone your age to meet people? I thought it was just us oldies who struggled."

"No, not really."

Aha! She'd met someone.

"It's easier for you oldies too now, with technology."

"If you think you're putting an app on my phone which buzzes whenever a single man is nearby, think again."

Instead she showed me a dating website.

"They all seem so perfect it makes me wonder what they're hiding," I said.

"So suspicious!"

"Come on. They're all quite good looking, have a great sense of humour and sound interesting. Why are they single?"

"It's hard for oldies to meet people, you said it yourself."

I regretted using that expression.

"Look at you, Mum. Attractive, fun, kind, good cook…"

"Flatterer! But yes, that's what it would say on a site like this. Then they'd meet me, find out the bad points and be disappointed. Like the men Sheila introduces me to. She builds them up so much that, however pleasant they are really, they're a huge disappointment."

"So if I tell you about an overweight bald bloke, with bad breath, a laugh like a stuttering donkey, seven ex-wives and obsessive interest in diesel trains, you'd beg to be introduced?"

"Perhaps not… but at least I wouldn't be disappointed if I did meet him."

She nodded.

"Thing is, I don't want to be introduced to anyone that way. There's too much pressure on both of us and I know we'd be looking for the snags."

"OK, but if you did just happen to meet someone nice, you'd look for the good points and give it a go?"

"Yes, I suppose…"

"And you could maybe join in some things to increase your chances? An evening class, or club or something?"

"Yes," I said with more enthusiasm. Whether or not

Carmel had met someone, and I was sure she had, she wouldn't stay living at home forever. It would be nice for me to get out and make friends and would get Sheila off my back; I could say I was following Carmel's dating advice. There was even a tiny possibility I'd meet someone I liked and who liked me back.

"And if *you* meet someone," I said, "Don't go worrying about me."

"Deal."

Not surprisingly it wasn't long before Carmel told me she wanted to bring Andy home.

"After what you said, I'm not going to build him up."

"Good idea and I promise to look only for positives."

"Thanks, Mum. Well, there's an age gap, he's a bit geeky and… it's not exactly a negative, but you've met him already."

Who could she mean?

She was right about the age gap and geekiness. Andrew used to be her maths teacher; I'm positive there was nothing going on then.

He presented me with a bunch of orange daisies and chatted like an old friend. What made it awkward was that I'd liked him a lot. Thankfully I'd hidden that.

It wasn't difficult to see Andrew in a positive light. He's attractive, intelligent and amusing. He has a good job, he's patient and polite. Why did he have to be the only male in the area Sheila hadn't tried to fix me up with?

The doorbell rang.

"I'll get it," I said as I made my escape.

I opened the door to a pleasant looking young man.

"Mum," Carmel said from right behind me. "I'd like you to meet Andy."

"Andy?" Of course that's what she'd said he was called. "But what about Andrew?"

"He's nice isn't he?" She winked. "Aunt Sheila said you'd like him. Now get the kettle on and slice some cake. I want you to make a good impression."

18. Cats And Dogs

Mel was about to apply a fresh coat of polish to her nails when she noticed movement outside the open window. A sleek black cat stepped daintily through. With one graceful movement it launched itself onto the settee. It paused for just a moment before settling itself on her lap.

"Hello there," Mel said to the beautiful creature. "Looks like the raspberry crush will have to wait." She screwed the top back on the polish bottle and made a fuss of her uninvited visitor.

"Were you talking to me?" Julian looked up from his phone. "Ah, I guess not. That was Carlos on the phone. He's invited us over for a pool party on Sunday, so we'll have to go to your mum's next week instead."

Another party! Mel didn't comment, she knew what the response would be. It was true that being seen there might help Julian's career, and Mum would hide her disappointment.

Julian stroked the cat. "You know, I always had you down as more of a dog person."

It was odd the way people said that, as though you were only allowed to like either cats or dogs, not both. Mel liked all animals.

Julian stretched his lean body. "Right, I'm off for a shower."

He was rather like a cat in some ways, Mel thought. He was always grooming himself and could be a little selfish.

Maybe that was harsh. Self-centred was more like it and she knew appearance was important in the entertainment industry.

He bought her gifts; silky underwear he'd like to see her in or wine he wanted to help drink. So like a cat bringing back its prey. It had enjoyed hunting the mouse so couldn't see the owner might not like to wake with it on their pillow. Actually she'd rather not have had cat hair on her skirt, but it was already too late. She'd have to change.

Julian had wandered into her life much as the cat had. He'd wanted a comfortable home so he'd moved himself in. It wasn't that he'd pressurised her or she hadn't wanted him around, but it hadn't occurred to him she might prefer to stay living alone. Or favour marriage over their more casual relationship.

The cat left as quickly and effortlessly as it had arrived. As Mel hastily scrambled into a hair free skirt, she wondered if she'd see it again. Perhaps it would visit often and she'd start thinking of it as hers. Then one day he'd see another open window and climb in there instead. Mel wasn't just thinking of the cat. She wasn't sure she'd ever be able to fully trust Julian.

He didn't mean to hurt her, but that evening Mel found herself alone in a crowded room. It often happened. Whenever Julian came across someone else he wanted to talk to, Mel would be forgotten as he flirted or tried to make useful contacts. He was always apologetic when he remembered and returned to her side with a drink and funny story. He'd kiss her cheek, hold her hand or lead her onto the dance floor. Very like a cat which had been out all night, rubbing itself affectionately around the ankles of its owner when it remembered who opened the cans of tuna.

"Morning, Mel. Coffee?" a colleague called as soon as she arrived at work the next day.

"Please."

Tom bounded off to fetch it. He'd bring it back as quickly as possible. He always wanted to please and was overenthusiastic about everything, just like a puppy.

"There you are!" He hardly sloshed any onto her desk.

"Thank you." Mel gave him her most charming smile.

He returned it, but there was no invitation behind his grin. There never would be. Most of the women in the office had tried to flirt with Tom, but he didn't respond. He was loyal to his girlfriend. Mel wanted someone like that.

That night she told Julian she'd be going to her mum's as arranged on Sunday and that she'd like him to look for somewhere else to live.

"But why, Mel?"

"You were right. I'm not really a cat person."

19. Frizzy Redhead Would Like To Meet…

"Good things will happen today," I tell myself before I get out of bed each morning and I'm always right, even if the good things are small and take a bit of looking for on occasion. No matter what happens I do try to be optimistic, to look for a bright side to any situation and hope for the best. I'm sure that's healthier than worrying about things which might never happen and not risking something which could bring us joy for fear it would go wrong.

Even so, at 7.23 AM, I already had that Monday morning feeling. Looking around at the gloomy faces of my fellow commuters convinced me I wasn't alone in that. Most had put up some kind of barrier. Headphones, constant tapping on smartphones or newspapers shaken out and pointedly angled away from those sitting alongside. It seemed they were all reading or listening to bad news. Those who had only their thoughts to occupy them didn't look any happier.

Why was everyone apparently so miserable? OK, so it was raining. That does more to make my red hair frizz and fill the train with a wet dog fragrance than to raise anyone's spirits, but surely some of us had things to be cheerful about. Using myself as an example I thought it through. I'd had a good weekend visiting with family. That included playing games with my brother's three boys so I got plenty of fresh air and exercise. As a result I'd slept well the previous night. When I told myself good things would happen I had no trouble believing it and had been quite happy when I got out of bed. I'd enjoyed a good breakfast of fruit, high fibre cereal and fresh coffee and been looking forward to the day ahead when I left home. That happiness seemed to have been sucked out of me somewhere between my front door and the tube. Why? If I could work it out I could put it right, perhaps for others as well as myself.

I continued my self analysis. Although I was a woman who's no longer really young and perky and who never did look like a fashion model, I was comfortable in my own skin. I wasn't famous or hugely important, yet still commanded a certain amount of respect. My job was generally rewarding. There was the satisfaction of knowing I always tried, and sometimes succeeded, in helping people. Plus there was salt and pepper guy. I meant his hair by that description, still thick but with a scattering of white hairs amongst the black; not that he was the sort to eat in a crowded carriage. About my age, not handsome exactly but nice to look at. He didn't smile a great deal on the train, but had the kind of face which looks as though it smiled a lot. (I really hoped he interpreted my own lines and creases in that way!) The smile when it did come was slightly lopsided and totally lovely. I knew because sometimes he'd given it when he'd happened to catch me glance in his direction. Him smiling at me again was one of the good things I hoped, believed, might happen that day.

So as I boarded the train I should have been happy, optimistic even. Probably I was when I approached the station. All those sad faces, grey in the early morning light, and all those sombre clothes, either that way to start with or darkened by the rain, sapped the joy from me. And I was one of the lucky ones; I'd remembered to pick up fresh milk the day before, I was healthy, could afford decent food and somewhere to live. There was my job and family. Who knew what some of these people battled? Perhaps there was perfectly good cause for the gloom radiating from some of them, but surely not all.

Probably it was unfair, certainly it was unkind, but I began to resent them spoiling my good humour. I was irritated by the fact that later in the day they, or people like them, would come into my place of work and drip their discontent all over me. I didn't include those with real problems who needed my help and would act upon my advice, but those who didn't seem to want to help themselves. Not many were like that thankfully, but those few were the hardest to assist.

'Stop this,' I mentally chided myself. 'Look for the good things, find the bright side.' As soon as the thought entered my head, I spotted a glimpse of brightness.

One girl stood out from the others on the train. It was partly her shiny pink boots, but more her hat with its array of woollen flowers. I'm not sure if they were knitted or crocheted but they were certainly bright. In common with half the train she was flicking through the free paper so I felt it was OK to watch her. Why not? She was the least miserable thing in view and I'd not yet spotted salt and pepper guy. The girl's expressions went through a rapid series from surprised to thoughtful to amused. She looked up and around her and then grinned as though recognising a friend. Whoever she was looking at wasn't visible to me until she gestured at the paper in an enquiring manner, presumably got a response, and beckoned him over.

There was just time for me to glimpse the boy's floppy hair and hopeful look before I busied myself with my own copy of the paper. Mostly that was to stop myself staring at them, but it soon occurred to me to hunt for whatever had got them together. Those personal ads were the obvious place to start and it didn't take me long to read *'Pink boots girl, maybe we could walk together? Dodgy green trainer man.'* To me he looked some years short of being a man but his footwear was certainly green and dodgy looking. And yes, I know because although I didn't actually stare, they drew my attention again. Not just mine, quite a few people were watching the young couple who were now chatting away, or maybe flirting is more accurate. There was some giggling, they stood closer even than the crowded conditions demanded. There was a great deal of playing with their own hair interspersed with lightly touching the other person's arm or playfully slapping their shoulder.

There were mixed reactions from the audience. All, I felt, were positive in some way, even those who were just cynically amused or feeling smug for, like me, having checked the paper and discovered what was going on. A good thing had happened, just as I'd said it would.

I shared the little anecdote at work, raising a small chuckle from my colleague. I reckon we both faced the day's workload just a little more cheerfully as a result. That got me thinking on the journey home. One brief message in the paper had brought happiness to the couple. Sure mismatched footwear wasn't a guaranteed basis for a lifelong relationship, but it might work out. Or they might enjoy some time together before deciding it wasn't meant to be. Those of us who shared the carriage with them were temporarily cheered and I probably wasn't the only person who'd passed that feeling on to the people I came into contact with that day. It was possible the happy ripples of that small incident had spread a long way.

What we needed was for more pebbles to be thrown into the pond. That newspaper message was, it seemed, a gift sent to brighten a miserable Monday. Maybe a higher power caused it to happen, but She wasn't the only being who had a hand in things. Dodgy trainer guy had actually written the message, or more likely tapped it into a smart phone and emailed it off. He wouldn't do anything like it again, not for a while anyway. Other people would and maybe the result would be the same. It wouldn't happen where I could see it though, would it?

An increase in happiness would be good for anyone, anywhere, but selfishly I wanted it to happen where I personally would benefit. Well, if you want something done, do it yourself. I studied those around me and sent in appropriate messages. Or maybe they were a touch inappropriate in some cases. Anyway, I sent them.

'Curly haired man in orange day-glow jacket and supermarket girl with plaits, I've seen you smile at each other. Why not say hi?' and *'Lady in red coat with flower brooch, that new hair style really suits you'* and *'Very shy boy with spots, there's someone who really likes you'*. There were a lot of shy boys with spots and I was sure someone did like most of them even if it was their mum, and believing they were likeable would go some way to allowing them to show that was really the case.

I hesitated over my choice of nickname for myself. My name is Debbie Rose and I nearly settled for just my initials, but decided something a bit more interesting might improve the chances of publication and chose Dr Happiness.

Every day I observed the passengers and sent something to the paper. They weren't all published and not all got a reaction, or at least not one I was there to see, but often my tiny effort was rewarded with a huge smile, or small grin, or a couple talking to each other. Whenever I felt a bit down, especially at work, I'd remind myself I was Dr Happiness with the power to make some lives a little better. It helped me deal with the times I felt powerless, when the good things were hard to see.

I began to enjoy the commute to work far more than I'd thought possible. On Monday mornings I was eager to see if pink boot girl and dodgy green trainer man were still a couple, to look out for other people I could write messages for, and to risk a glance at salt and pepper guy. Almost always when I looked in his direction he was looking in mine. Sometimes he frowned as though wanting to ask what I was doing. I'm sure it was that and not just concern I might turn out to be a stalker. Sometimes he gestured at the paper just as pink boots girl had to green trainers when she'd started me off on this whole thing.

The obvious thing to do was send another message to the paper. I did. '*Salt and pepper guy, if you want to know what I'm doing, why not ask?*' This time instead of Dr Happiness I signed it '*frizzy redhead*'. I had to send a version of that three times before it was printed and the day it was, salt and pepper guy wasn't in the same carriage.

He saw it though and came to find me. "I think I've worked it out," he said. "You're Dr Happiness, aren't you?"

I admitted it.

"I like your name for me… I'm hoping I am salt and pepper guy?"

"You are."

"Sounds so much better than 'going grey'. I'm not keen on yours though, for one thing your hair is curly not frizzy… on dry days anyway."

I was pretty sure then that we'd get along for more than

just one train journey.

"So, Dr Happiness, do you have a prescription for me?" he asked.

"What you need is a nice meal out and some cheerful red-headed company," I said, my voice far more confident than the rest of me.

"In that case, will you come to dinner with me tonight?"

That wasn't a good thing to happen. It was a really, really, good thing. Obviously I said yes; us doctors know what's good for us as well as our patients. I grinned all the way to the clinic and dispensed soppy smiles all day.

20. What He Wanted

Valerie knew it had been a comfort to her husband, in his last weeks, to know they'd started to put their plans into action. Well, his plans really. It was Frank who'd worked it all out. They'd sell their house which was too big for them. That would allow them to give their daughter some money for the business she wanted to set up and leave them enough for a bungalow in town. They'd then be closer to the shops and on a bus route. They could get an allotment. Unlike their corner plot it wouldn't be under constant public scrutiny, so could be gardened in a more relaxed manner. Frank would grow a few vegetables and Valerie could have flowers to pick. They could go on holidays.

Valerie decided to go ahead with the plan. It would be a comfort to know she was doing what Frank wanted and would keep her busy. She needed that.

Bridget was relieved about her mum's decision. Yes, partly because of the money. That would be a real help. Mostly though she was pleased because it would be good for Mum. She really needed something definite to do and of course it was sensible not to be struggling on her own with the big house and garden. It was good she'd be closer to Bridget too.

Valerie, to her surprise, rather enjoyed having people come to view the house. For one thing she got to talk to people about something other than her loss. The people thinking of buying the house were couples hoping to raise a family and wouldn't want to associate the house with that.

Better instead to tell them about all her happy memories there. Better too, to be thinking about them.

It was almost fun to look round smaller properties with Bridget in the hope of finding somewhere she'd like to live. Valerie couldn't really picture herself being happy anywhere without Frank, but putting on a brave face for Bridget helped her feel a little more positive. It was hard not to accept she might have a future whilst she was working towards creating it.

Bridget thought helping pack up all her parents' things would be depressing, but it wasn't as bad as she'd feared. Mum was determined to be positive and they had quite a laugh over old photos and memories. Mum kept Dad's best gardening tools.

"It's not just sentimentality, love. I intend to use them."

It was so reassuring to see her looking forward.

Bridget found a note from Dad, addressed to her, tucked away where she was likely to see it among his financial papers. She slipped it into her pocket to read when she was alone.

'*Hello, love,*' it began. '*I hope I've not left all the bank stuff in a mess for you to sort out for your mum. I'm guessing she'll have asked you to help as you've always been clever at that sort of thing*'. He went on to explain the plans he'd made with Valerie. '*I think it would be for the best for her to continue with them, but she isn't to do so if her circumstances change or she just doesn't want to.*'

It was written so much as Dad used to speak that Bridget had to keep wiping away tears as she read. Should she show Mum? Dad had addressed it to her, so must have trusted her to decide. Mum was coping brilliantly so far. The letter might upset her. Also Mum wasn't very decisive. She might just drift without her positive plans for the future. No, Bridget would keep it for the time being.

Valerie received an offer for the house and began seriously looking for a bungalow. Within days she was shown one exactly like Frank had described their new home. There was a bit of garden front and back which she could tend if she felt like it, or have grassed over if not. It was a lovely modern place that would be easy to keep clean. The shops were just a short walk away and from what she'd seen the neighbours were very friendly. It was ideal, except of course that Frank wasn't there to share it with her.

Both sales were going through with little trouble. Bridget was delighted. She almost had the money for her business and her mother settled close by, in a home she could manage herself. It was all very convenient; for Bridget. Was she being fair to Mum encouraging her to keep on with Dad's plans? She'd got her managerial skills, or bossiness depending on your point of view, from her Dad. Mum should do what she wanted, not what suited Bridget best.

"You don't have to do this, Mum. It's not too late to change your mind."

"I want to, love. It's what your dad wanted and really I am looking forward to living in the bungalow. If I can be happy anywhere without your dad, I think I shall be there."

Once again Bridget decided not to show her the letter. When Mum moved in Bridget was sure she'd acted correctly. As Mum chose wallpaper and hemmed matching curtains, she seemed almost back to her old self.

Valerie settled in very quickly, partly thanks to her new neighbour Stuart. When she mentioned her hopes of getting an allotment he took her to see his own huge plot.

"I'm not sure I could dig all that!" she said.

"They are big. I grow loads more veg than I need. Would you like some of these greens?"

"Please. They'd be lovely in a bit of bubble and squeak with a chop."

"Sounds good. I'm not much of a cook myself."

Valerie began cooking his produce for both of them a couple of times a week. Stuart suggested she have a corner of his allotment to grow her flowers. She accepted and planted sunflowers and dahlias; bright colours ideal for picking. Everything was working out and she got on so well with Stuart it was almost as if meeting him were part of the plan.

She still loved Frank of course and sometimes sat holding his photo with a tear rolling down her cheek, but mostly she tried to focus on happy memories. It was a blessing she didn't have to look at his empty chair or suffer aching loneliness. She had a new home, new friends and a new life. Frank's plans had worked brilliantly. He'd have loved all this. Bridget's business was doing so well too. Frank would have been proud.

Valerie was shopping in town when Stuart saw her and suggested they have coffee and cake. Valerie had almost forgotten that eating out more was on Frank's list. She'd not have felt comfortable going into the coffee shop on her own, but enjoyed it with Stuart. It became a regular weekly treat, then twice weekly as the winter weather meant they spent less time on the allotment. One day as they began the walk home, Stuart noticed a sign in the travel agent's for a remarkably inexpensive cruise to the Caribbean.

"Be nice that, wouldn't it?" He didn't actually suggest they went together, but Valerie felt a hint of that was in the background.

Could she go on holiday with Stuart? To get a good deal they'd have to share a cabin, but she wasn't sure she'd be happy in one on her own anyway. They could have twin beds... What would Bridget think though? Would she mind, think she was betraying Frank? And what about Frank, was it wrong to carry on his plans without him? Was she using Stuart to do that?

Valerie spoke to her daughter. "I'm worried about your dad's list."

"It's OK, Mum. If you don't want to continue with it you don't have to."

"That's the problem. I feel guilty for carrying on with it."

"And I've been feeling guilty for encouraging you. It fitted in so well with what I wanted."

"It would have done. Your father was very good at making plans and I suppose I've always been good at following them."

"Yes, with a bit of prompting from me, I confess."

"Oh?"

"Yes. Remember when you both decided to help raise money for that charity. Dad was hoping you'd bake lots of cakes that he could sample. Instead you donated half his wardrobe to their jumble sale."

"That's right. If I remember rightly you bought me cake making books and loads of biscuit cutters at the same sale and were as good as your father at the cake sampling. So you were in on the plot, were you?"

"Yes. That's what's worrying me now. That I've bullied you into following Dad's plans."

"You've not bullied me, love and neither did your father. I went along with his plans because they were either exactly what I wanted to do anyway, or I could see they were the sensible course of action. If I'd really not wanted to, I'd have said. But I do want to… it just seems so wrong to be doing it without him. No, it's worse than that, I'm doing them with someone else. Stuart and I are sharing his allotment just like your father and I planned we would."

"That's OK, Mum. It's just a sensible idea and Stuart is lovely. Dad would have liked him and as he can't be gardening with you I think he'd be pleased you weren't doing it alone."

"It's not just the gardening. We have coffee and cake every week and I cook his Sunday lunch."

"Oh, Mum!" Bridget hugged her. "I'm pleased for you. Really, it's nothing to feel guilty about. It's not as though you've forgotten Dad, is it?"

"No, but it feels wrong."

"Well, I should think so. Coffee indeed! I suppose it's one of those fancy ones with a silly name like lattice or caps and chinos or something?"

Valerie laughed. "You sounded just like your dad saying that. You're right though, he'd have hinted, none too subtly, that a nice pot of tea was a better plan."

"And would you have drunk tea?"

"Perhaps I would at that. I do like the coffee…"

"Keep drinking it then. You don't have to do everything Dad… but that's not what you're saying is it?"

"No. I feel guilty carrying on your Dad's plans with another man. Stuart and I… well there's a possibility of us going on holiday together."

"Go if you want to, Mum. Lots of people have holidays, you know and Dad didn't plan theirs."

"I suppose not."

"Dad left me a note. I found it when you were getting ready to move. I don't have it with me but I've read it several times wondering if I should tell you. I can pretty much remember most of it. I think he'd guessed he didn't have much time left."

"I did wonder. We discussed all his plans of course, but towards the end he explained much more of the detail and instead of those funny little notes he used to make himself he started writing everything out in full. It's been easy to follow them. I guess he said I didn't have to do that?"

"He did. But he also said he'd be happy if you did. That he wanted you to be happy if that was possible and that he thought his plans might be the right thing for you alone as well as you both together."

"I see. Thank you, love. That does sound like him."

"He didn't mention Stuart obviously, but there was something about me supporting you in whatever choices you made and to remember you're a woman in your own right, not just one half of my parents. Like I said, I think he'd like that you had Stuart for company."

"He was a good man, your dad. I'm not so sure I'd have been happy for him to be making plans with another woman, though I suppose that would be better than him not making them for anyone. To give up and … yes, a lot better. Thanks, love. I'm going to plan a holiday."

"Great. Where to? Dad always fancied seeing the pyramids and all those ancient tombs, I remember. I'm not sure Egypt is the best place to visit at the moment though."

"I don't want to go there. That's one of your father's plans I wouldn't have gone along with! All that dust and long coach journeys and climbing down into confined spaces.

No, I'm going on a cruise."

Bridget laughed.

"I suppose it's ironic in a way. Sailing was a plan of your father's that didn't work no matter how hard he tried. Remember all those trips we planned and they went wrong? Ferry crossings to France which we didn't take because he got tickets for that awful tunnel at a bargain price and when he booked our trip down the Thames and accidentally got us on the London eye instead?"

"That's right. I'm sure your plan will be more successful." Bridget didn't explain that her dad's had been too. He got horribly seasick when he'd been on a school trip and had schemed to never go on any kind of ship or boat ever again.

"Oh it will. Thanks so much for listening love. It's a great comfort to know I really am doing exactly what your dad would have wanted as we sail around the Caribbean."

21. Becoming Best

Ellie had always been better than her twin Bea. That's how it seemed to Bea. They looked just the same so she wasn't prettier and they'd both passed the same number of exams (although Ellie had got one more A*) and got equally good jobs. But Ellie was just that bit more… confident was it? Or had her extra confidence come from realising she was better than her sister? Ellie walked first, talked first, got more badges in Brownies than her twin. .

Bea told herself she was stupid to feel like that. They were both healthy, happy, loved and both nice girls. They were the same in lots of ways, even names, as Bea was Beatrice Eleanor and Ellie was Eleanor Beatrice. And they were both Swathlings of the famous Swathling dynasty.

Ellie was engaged to a lovely man called Sebastien while Bea's boyfriend was clearly not entirely sure he wanted to propose. She knew Chris had spoken to her father because Dad told her. She knew Chris had bought a ring because Ellie had helped him choose it; just as Ellie's fiancé had asked Bea to help him. Would they be the same? They might as the twins had similar tastes in a lot of things. Bea grinned; if Ellie had the best taste then Bea would get the best ring. Still, it wouldn't be her that was best and it didn't look like she was going to get the ring on her finger anyway.

Chris asked, "What's wrong?"

Bea couldn't say she was worried he wouldn't propose as

she didn't want to pressurise him into it. Instead she said, "I want to be better than my sister for once."

Chris looked really unhappy.

"Don't look so worried," Bea said. "I'm not really jealous and moody and all that. I'm happy with my life."

"Even your boyfriend?"

"Of course!"

"But I'm not really good enough for you. I hoped I was because you care for me but I'm no match for Sebastien. He's richer, smarter, taller."

"Richer? Yes, he has a better paid job but you can't tell me that being a banker is better than being a teacher. That brings rewards money can't buy."

"I suppose."

"And yes, Sebastien is taller but that's not a good thing. Everyone notices him." His height drew attention to him and Ellie. Bea didn't enjoy being the centre of attention that way. Sebastien was the best husband for Ellie, Chris was best for Bea – if he'd only propose!

Bea decided she wouldn't allow their respective insecurities to cause them another moment's unhappiness. "I suppose Sebastien is slightly smarter than you though. He worked out for himself he'd won the love of a Swathling girl. Looks like you need a hint. Chris, will you marry me?"

"Yes!"

The rings weren't quite the same, but very similar. Neither was better than the other. The same was true of the dresses and honeymoon destinations they chose. They were better suited to each girl but not actually better.

"Bea," Ellie said one day. "I don't want to detract from your special day… but I was wondering… how do you feel about a double wedding?"

"Yes! Let's do that." Bea would be free of any nagging doubt Ellie's wedding was better than hers.

She asked Chris if he'd mind sharing the day.

"I'll be marrying the best girl in the world, nothing else really matters."

"That's so sweet, and I think you mean it and aren't just making me feel better, although it does. I know I'm silly about this but I'm not the best sister, just most suited to you. If you were Seb you'd like Ellie more, wouldn't you?"

"I see what you mean but I'm not Seb. But don't worry about who's the best Swathling twin now you're about to become the very best Mrs Thompson."

"Ah."

"What?"

"You know we're the last of the Swathlings? Well, Granddad asked us to keep our surnames. Could we double barrel them?"

"It'd be an honour to add your family name to mine."

"Which way round? Swathling-Thompson? Thompson-Swathling? No that sounds like an insurance firm."

"Swathling-Thompson it is then." Chris laughed.

"What?"

"You'll see!"

On the morning of the wedding, Chris sent her a box on which he'd written, 'It's what you've always been, but today we make it official.' Inside was a gorgeous locket engraved with her new initials; B.E.S.T.

22. Turning The Tables

Wonderful as it was, the sight of Skye's Cuillin mountains soaring up in front of them couldn't raise Moll's spirits. She just couldn't work out what was wrong with Douglas. Until a few days ago she'd thought she knew him almost as well as she knew herself, but clearly that wasn't the case. Something was troubling him and she had no idea what. He was doing his best to hide it, but now and then a worried frown appeared and he checked his phone more frequently than usual. She'd asked straight out if he was worried about his health or that of anyone in the family, or concerned over money or work. Each time he'd said no and she'd believed him.

"Is it me, then? Or… someone else?"

"Don't be daft, Moll! You know I love you. Everything is fine."

She believed that too, all except the last three words. Something was definitely making him unhappy. She stopped asking though, as that seemed to be adding to the problem.

It couldn't be this trip could it? She'd thought he'd be in his element. Douglas was what's known as a ferry enthusiast, although ferry obsessive would be nearer the mark. He photographed as many as he possibly could and subscribed to *Ship's Monthly* magazine and visited the *Maritime Photographic* website at least once a week. Most of their previous trips had involved looking at ferries, at least for part of the time.

She'd never complained because in truth she didn't mind. Moll was pleased he had a hobby which took them to interesting places and they always spent plenty of time doing other things too. Douglas made time for a good look round any gardens or natural beauty spots nearby. They admired the local birdlife and laughed at their usually unsuccessful attempts to capture the feathered creatures on camera.

"Why is it they stay still right up until I get them in focus?" Molly wondered.

"Someone should make them issue timetables!" Douglas had replied.

It was a standing joke among their family that any collection of holiday pictures always included a patch of ground or a twig where an attractive bird had been just a fraction of a second before. Not many people realised the tradition had begun on honeymoon. Moll and Douglas had watched entranced as a fabulous bird soared above them.

"It's an eagle," Moll had said. She'd spoken quietly, as though the sound of her voice might disturb it.

"I booked it just for you," Douglas had joked, speaking just as softly.

It wasn't until nearly too late they thought of trying to get a photograph. When it was developed, all anyone could see was a tiny black speck, but to Moll and Douglas it was a treasured image. The magnificent animals had been even rarer back then and seeing one on their honeymoon had seemed like a good omen.

Whether it had anything to do with the bird or not they'd had forty wonderful years, sharing their lives and growing ever closer. During that time, Moll had asked Douglas to teach her to take photographs.

"Great idea, love. That way when a ferry comes in we can each be in a different location. If the sun isn't right for one of us, or there's something in the way the other might have more luck."

"Actually, I was thinking of taking pictures of our garden and the flowers we see when we go away."

"Ah."

"I suppose I could snap the odd ferry, if you're really nice to me," she'd teased Douglas.

"I'm always nice to you."

"That's true."

And it was. He was a wonderful husband in so many ways, including indulging her passion for everything floral. Douglas was patient when she spent hours browsing garden centres and plant nurseries, even if he did sometimes leave her to it and find a comfy spot to study ferry timetables. Still, this time the holiday was to celebrate their fortieth wedding anniversary and he'd promised it would all be for her. That didn't seem quite fair to Moll as it was his anniversary too, so she'd chosen a location which should please them both.

"I'd like to go to the Isle of Skye," she'd declared.

"Are you sure? Not Versailles, Monet's garden at Giverny? Or …"

"The hanging gardens of Babylon? No. Now you've taught me to take photos, I thought I'd 'collect' wild flowers of Scotland and do a talk for the gardening club. Maybe I'll even photograph an eagle!"

He'd grinned at that and immediately begun searching for holiday accommodation on the island. She'd known she could leave that to him. Douglas knew the sort of places she'd like to say, and Moll, in looking up the locations of the ferry ports, as well as more usual places of interest, had discovered the island was small enough that they could travel from anywhere to anywhere in the same day.

What Moll hadn't told Douglas was that she remembered how he sighed wistfully whenever he saw pictures of Caledonian MacBrayne ferries and so had chosen a location where several of them, plus the elusive birds they both so admired, were to be found. As soon as they'd decided the dates of the trip, Moll had gone onto the internet and looked up details of wildlife tours. She was delighted to learn that there were not one, but two species of eagle on Skye; Golden and White-tailed Sea Eagles. The timing of their trip was perfect, as that's when the eagles would be feeding their chicks, and so regularly in the same area and far easier to spot than usual. Special boat tours were offered, on which views of the eagles were almost guaranteed. Douglas would love it as much as she would, Moll was sure. The only snag was that lots of other people had discovered it was the perfect time to take an eagle watching trip. Every ticket, for the entire week, was sold out.

"I can put you on the waiting list," she was told.

"Please do." At the time Moll had been confident that someone would drop out in the weeks before their trip, but she'd heard nothing.

Other than Moll's slight disappointment that it didn't seem likely they'd get to see the eagles, the first part of their holiday had gone really well. They'd been on some lovely walks, including the steep climb up to the Old Man of Storr. Getting up there had been hard work, but well worth it for the amazing views. Of course they'd taken pictures and the huge piece of upright rock had stayed obligingly still. On another day they'd been to see the Fairy Pools, which had enchanted Moll – once she got there. First they had to cross stepping stones through a stream. The stream wasn't deep, but it was wide. The stones were solid and plenty big enough for her feet, but they were a good stride apart and seemed quite high.

Douglas had taken one look at them and squeezed her hand. "You'll be fine, love. Let's watch how people do it and then we can follow them over."

Bless him, he knew she'd be nervous and would need a moment to get her confidence up. They'd watched a few people go over, including a small girl and her father carrying a baby in a backpack.

"Come on then," Douglas said, taking her hand and pulling her gently towards the stream.

"There's a group coming back down," Moll pointed out.

"Best hurry then."

In trying not to hold anyone up, Moll forgot some of her nerves and she was able to follow Douglas's sure footed lead.

"Well done, love!" he said when she reached the opposite bank.

They'd taken lots of pictures of water flowing in and out of the pretty pools and Moll had photographed flowers there and everywhere else they'd visited.

Until this trip Douglas had not had a single Caledonian MacBrayne ferry picture in his collection and they'd already bagged four on the journey to Scotland and another two on the island. He was especially pleased to realise each one was different, ranging from one which only had space for ten cars, up to one as large as the ones they'd once seen going out from Portsmouth to the Isle of Wight.

Each morning of the trip, Douglas had asked her to pick a destination and she'd programmed the sat nav for a route which included places she wanted to see as well as one of the tiny and picturesque ferry ports which dotted the Scottish coast. Where possible she'd timed the journey to coincide with a Caledonian MacBrayne arrival or departure. It had been fun working it out and surprising him.

"Oh! Look, Moll, a CalMac!" he'd exclaimed the first time.

"Hmm and it looks as though you'll be just in time to get a picture. Off you go."

"Are you sure?"

"Go or you'll miss it!"

He'd happily obeyed and she'd wandered about getting her own pictures of wild flowers growing nearby. She'd known of course that garden heathers came in lots of different forms and colours but hadn't expected to see almost as much variety amongst the wild plants. Most of the ports were really just a tiny car park and a slipway, so even there she was out in the countryside. Sometimes Douglas dropped her off at a remote beach where the ferry would pass close by, or up on a cliff somewhere to get a long shot. She'd loved that; sitting in the sunshine watching the birds swoop above gorgeous scenery and being able to carefully study the delicate blue harebells, pink achillea, acres of multi-hued heathers and other native wildflowers as she waited for him to come back for her.

It should all have been perfect but Douglas clearly wasn't happy. The more ferries they saw the worse it seemed to get. He hadn't gone off them; he couldn't keep the hope from his voice as he asked her to check the timetable she'd picked up in the first port, nor his delight when yet again they 'just happened' to be in the right place at the right time. It was after he'd got his pictures and spent a few minutes enthusing that his voice trailed off and a worried look clouded his face. Moll didn't know what to do.

Would seeing the old turntable ferry at Kylerhea cheer him up? She'd read it was the last one still running in Scotland and it certainly looked unusual. Cars drove on and then were swung round like spice jars on the lazy Susan in her cupboard. Surely he'd like to see that, or would it be the last straw? She was beginning to wonder if she knew her husband at all. As she switched on the sat nav and hesitated over typing in the location, Douglas made his own suggestion.

"Let's go to Moll. I saw a place with that name on the map. It doesn't look very big, but we could get a photo of you by the 'welcome to Moll' sign to go with the one of me in Douglas."

"Lovely." She tried to sound enthusiastic even though from a glance at the map it seemed there wouldn't be much to see. They'd had a good time on that trip a few years back and Douglas had been delighted with the Isle of Man steam packet ferries. Maybe going to Moll would help him recapture that happiness.

Moll programmed the sat nav and they travelled through gorgeous scenery for several miles, with her chattering brightly about how nice it would be to go somewhere which shared her name. She couldn't resist asking Douglas to pull over a couple of times so she could photograph a mountain swirled with mist, a tumbling waterfall and an attractive grouping of trees. Each time he got out the car too and came to admire whatever had caught her attention. He definitely seemed to be brightening up. Then they spotted a sign informing them Moll was three miles away and Douglas took the appropriate turning.

The road was horrible; bumpy, narrow with few passing places and so dusty it was difficult even to admire the view. Moll wasn't surprised Douglas had stopped smiling again.

"It seems longer than three miles," he remarked just after Moll realised the same thing. They couldn't have made a mistake though as there'd been no turnings to miss. Actually there'd been almost nothing at all, just one cottage and something they thought was connected with salmon fishing. Soon they were back on the main road. A sign, pointing in the direction they'd come, informed them Moll was three miles back.

"How odd," Moll said. "You'd think there would have been something to say we'd reached it. I suppose that cottage must have been it. Maybe there used to be more houses once?"

Douglas didn't reply until he'd pulled into a layby. "Moll, I'm so sorry. I realised it wasn't going to be a big town with lots of things to do, but I was expecting a village and a sign I could photograph you by at least, and I'd hoped for a café or something."

He sounded really upset. Moll wished she'd not tried so hard to sound enthusiastic about her namesake.

"Come on, Douglas. It's not your fault there was nothing there."

"It's not just that. The whole trip was supposed to be for you. We always do what I want and this was going to be different but we've still ended up at ferry ports and I waste half the day there adding to my collection. I'd planned for us to go out to a really nice restaurant in Inverness for our anniversary and we won't be there in time."

Moll was glad now that she'd not heard back about the boat tour to see the eagles. If she'd told him she'd booked them in for that it would have confirmed his daft idea that he was letting her down on this trip.

"Silly man. Of course we always end up in ferry ports; I programme them into the sat nav!"

"Oh. Yes, I suppose you must have… That's really nice of you."

"Look, blow your nose and take a picture of me by the sign pointing to the place that never was. Once we've forgotten the awful drive we'll probably find it funny."

"All right." He gave a small smile. "Makes a change from photographing birds which aren't there." It was a brave attempt, but she could tell he was still unhappy.

He got her to pose with a map and Moll did her best to put on a 'feeling lost' expression. It wasn't difficult.

Afterwards, Moll said, "Right, now let's see if we can find a real village with a real café and get a cake."

Fortunately they spotted a tearoom within minutes.

"I'm just going to wash my hands. You order will you, Douglas?"

"OK, love. What would you like?"

"You know me well enough by now to get it right."

She was safe, even if he didn't actually know her mind any better than it seemed she knew his. She'd not yet found a kind of cake she didn't like. Sure enough by the time she'd freshened up, commandeered a table and sorted out her laptop he was back with a pot of tea, two tempting specimens of cake and a knife so they could have half of each.

"You do know me so well, Douglas. If I'd ordered the cakes I'd have got two different ones and a knife too."

He looked a little happier at that and his mood improved further as they enjoyed the strawberry layer and lemon drizzle cakes.

"Now, look at my photos." She set her laptop to run a slideshow of her best pictures. Some were of ferries, but more weren't. There lots of wild flowers, including close ups of individual blooms and wider views showing the conditions they were growing in. There were shots of the scenery, with and without Douglas. There were even some of a highland cow she'd 'stalked' when he was waiting for a ferry to load up and go out again. "I have done what I wanted," she told him.

"I'm glad and you've got some really good pictures. The gardening club will enjoy them, I'm sure."

"I'll enjoy showing them and I couldn't have taken them without you teaching me how." She reached for his hand.

He took hold of hers and squeezed it. "And you really don't mind about the ferries?"

"Not at all. Well…" She switched off her lap top.

"Well what?"

"It would be nice to go on one as a change from just looking at them. There's an old one not too far from here. You drive on and then you're swung round so you can drive off the other side."

"The turntable ferry Glenachulish? I'd love to see that. I wonder when it runs." He reached for his phone.

"That's the one. It runs from Kylerhea to Glenelg every twenty minutes between ten and six… " She trailed off as she realised that although Douglas was looking absolutely delighted, it was nothing to do with ferries, but the result of a text message on his phone.

"Moll, my love, as you're so keen to see that funny sounding ferry, I'll be happy to take you, but do you mind if we do something else tomorrow?"

"What do you have in mind?"

"A boat trip to see eagles! I tried to book it the day you said you wanted to come here, but it was full. I've been on a waiting list ever since and have just heard there's a space available for us."

"I can't think of anything I'd rather do, nor anyone I'd rather do it with."

"Same here, Moll my love. Same here."

23. Can't Do It Without You

Lee took a deep breath when his name was called, then strode onto the stage to collect something he fully deserved. Beaming delightedly he accepted the award for 'outstanding wildlife photography in the natural environment'. The trophy would look handsome on his mantelpiece, the cheque was welcome and the publicity could only be good for business. As the youngest ever winner he should get decent press coverage.

He thanked the judges, talked a little about his work, and said how proud he was. "I know my family and friends are too. They've always had faith in my abilities and supported me right from the start. I couldn't have done it without them. Especially you, Megan." To the delight of the audience, he blew her a kiss.

As soon as he could, he returned to his girlfriend's side. "Thank goodness that's over."

"You did brilliantly," Megan said. "And that bit at the end was so sweet."

"You tell me it's true often enough!"

"And so it is."

A passing waiter offered them champagne. They accepted with smiles, and clinked glasses. For a few minutes they chatted about the fascinating assignments he might gain as a result of the award. Their mood was as bubbly as the wine.

Once the glasses were empty, Megan said, "I think we

should mingle a bit – and talk to the press."

"Must we?"

"Afraid so."

She was right. Before she'd started coming to exhibitions and events with him, he'd kept to himself as much as possible and earned a reputation for being aloof, even arrogant. With Megan there, chattering away, it was far less noticeable that he hadn't a clue what to say in social situations.

After circulating for a while and repeating the same irritating conversations half a dozen times, Lee whispered, "excuse me a moment," and slipped away. He paced up and down outside, taking big breaths of cold air, hoping to cool his temper.

It was always like this. People wanted to know which camera he used, as though anyone could get results like his if they spent enough on their equipment. They told him how lucky he was with the light, or to have captured the precise moment an arctic hare leapt into the air, or an eagle swooped, after he'd spent days, sometimes weeks, camped out on location, watching and waiting.

"Amazing what you can do with computers these days, isn't it?" was uttered as though his software had a special filter to add in talent.

Two women came out, discussing his work.

"I can see why his pictures are so popular," one said.

"Lovely, aren't they? Wish I could get shots like that, but I can't even photograph my cat without cutting off his head."

Lee smiled, pleased at least some people realised it wasn't as easy as he made it look. He decided he should go back in and try to mingle again. As a prizewinner it would look odd if he didn't. It took a while to locate Megan as he'd not thought to look in the midst of a press swarm. Honestly, the way they were crowded round, with film cameras and microphones, anyone would think she was Prince Harry's wife, not his own perfectly ordinary Megan.

It seemed she felt a little the same way. "Without an h," he heard her say as he got closer.

"Nor an HRH," someone added. Megan's polite chuckle wasn't heard above the man laughing at his own weak joke.

"He said he couldn't do it without you. What do you have to say to that?" a reporter asked.

"It's perfectly true…"

Lee had heard enough and abruptly turned away. Was even Megan, who knew exactly how much effort he put in, belittling his achievements? Taking the credit? He'd been training for years and worked hard for long hours to get his incredible shots. Yes, she was his assistant and quite helpful, carrying equipment and passing him what he needed, but anyone could do that.

He found another waiter and grabbed a glass. The wine seemed to have lost its sparkle.

"Where did you get to?" Megan asked him, when she got away from the press.

"Who cares? It's not like I'm anyone important."

"You are to me," she said, reaching for his hand.

He felt bad about snapping at her then, but couldn't find the words to tell her so, not with first the crowd in the hall, and then the driver of the taxi listening in.

He probably should have kept quiet the next morning too, but in an effort to show why he'd been moody, he reminded her about some of the things he'd had to put up with the previous evening. "What makes it worse is that it came after I'd won that award. It's like nothing I do matters to anyone."

Megan looked suitably annoyed, on his behalf he assumed, so he let all his petty annoyances spill into her sympathetic ear.

"You're feeling unappreciated, is that it?" she asked.

"Yes, I suppose… "

"Me too! Last night you were being honoured and rewarded, yet you sulked while leaving me to deal with the press. Just like you leave me to pack up your gear and come running after you when your subject suddenly makes a move. Or to tidy the flat and cook dinner while you spend all your time processing images, or to sort out the details before your jobs and see to the invoicing afterwards."

"But you're my assistant. That's your job."

"I thought I was rather more than just an assistant."

"I couldn't do it without you, is that what you mean? Well, you're wrong, I can and I will."

He didn't need to see the tears in her eyes to know how unkind he'd been. It was shame, and anger with himself, which stopped him going to her until she'd already started packing a bag. It was shock which made him stand silent as she finished, and then left.

Lee tried to work, but it was hopeless. Even as he pressed the shutter he knew the results wouldn't be worth processing.

Over the next few days, things improved a little. He completed an assignment for a wildlife charity, but the clients were merely satisfied, not delighted. Lee wasn't even that. It was clear to him that he'd lost that something special, which lifted his work from just good enough to really good. The shots were technically OK, but he could do better. Or could have done once.

He'd only been truly good since he'd met his muse… Was Megan really that? Had that extra touch of talent came from her?

Lee dismissed that thought as he drove to the New Forest, hoping to photograph a deer giving birth. He and Megan had visited numerous times, watching the deer and getting to know their habits. Megan had researched deer births and contacted forest rangers to learn where newborn fawns were sighted, so he was able to set up a hide in the most likely spot. If they'd not rowed, Megan would now be by his side, pouring the coffee and handing him the cake she'd thought to bring. They couldn't have talked though and he wasn't particularly hungry, so he tried to convince himself it made little difference that she wasn't there.

The deer began fidgeting; something was about to happen. It turned, moving closer as it did, giving Lee a perfect view of the tiny feet just emerging. Any moment she'd give birth, and the action would be even closer than he'd anticipated. Lee reached out for the lens he knew Megan would have ready. She wasn't there. He had to momentarily look away and find it himself. It was no problem; he had it attached to the camera just in time to take a rapid succession of shots as the baby deer slithered onto the grass and took its first breaths. The pictures would be good, he knew. Among his best. So why wasn't he satisfied?

He took more photos as the mother licked her baby, of it staggering to its feet and then suckling. All the time he felt something was missing, wrong, empty. Maybe he was hungry after all?

After he'd waited for the deer and fawn to move away, he dismantled the hide, packed away his gear, and went to visit his mum. She knew him better than anyone; she'd reassure him he'd be just fine without Megan.

Mum had barely given him a hug before asking, "What's wrong, love? Where's Megan?"

He choked back a sob. "We've split up."

"Oh dear, I am sorry. Why did she go?"

"I said I didn't need her."

"What on earth for? She's a lovely girl and you seemed so happy."

"She's not perfect, you know."

"Unlike you, I suppose?"

"What does that mean?" he demanded.

"You can be a bit selfish, love. You're a very talented photographer, but you don't let anyone forget it, and you expect that poor girl to trail around everywhere after you, doing everything you don't want to be bothered with."

"I know, I know. She says the same and that I couldn't do it without her!"

"As a joke. And because she wants to be important in your life, for you to appreciate her."

"A joke?"

"You should have heard her at that award ceremony."

"I did," Lee told her.

"Don't think so, love. She was on her own; as you'd done your usual disappearing trick." Mum played the recording for him.

Just as he had on the night, Lee heard a man say, "Nor an

HRH," and laugh loudly at his own weak joke.

"He said he couldn't do it without you. What do you have to say to that?" a reporter asked.

"It's perfectly true…"

That was the point at which Lee had walked away. Now he heard the rest.

"… He did say that and I confess I often say it to him. It's not accurate though. He's a brilliant photographer and doesn't need me at all."

She gave a determined smile, but Lee could see sadness in her eyes. It was clear she believed her words and felt he didn't value her either as an assistant or as a girlfriend.

"I happen to think she's wrong," Mum said.

She probably meant that he couldn't do his job without her. That his lack of social skills meant he needed her to deal with customers and sweet talk them into obtaining access to the best locations. That he needed her to take care of the paperwork, flat and him, so he could concentrate just on his work and have the time he needed to do it.

Mum wouldn't know Megan was wrong about him not needing her in a different way, because he'd never told, or shown, anyone how he felt. He'd do it right now, but it wasn't Mum who needed to know. He called Megan and, very politely, asked if she'd meet him.

Just like him, Megan looked as though she'd not been sleeping well. She had that drawn look which had made Mum ask him what was wrong.

She kept her distance. "What is it, Lee?"

"I wanted to apologise for taking you for granted and not appreciating all you do for me." That was so easy to say he wondered why he'd not had the sense to do so before.

"You're admitting you can't do it without me?" She smiled, but there was a challenge in her voice.

"Work would be much harder and far less enjoyable, but I'd…" He could, quite truthfully, have informed her he'd taken some great shots that day. That's exactly how he'd have responded a week ago. But a week ago, he'd thought that was what was important.

"No, I can't do it without you. And I don't want to."

"Oh, Lee… "

"I don't just mean photography, Megan. It's everything; life, happiness. I really can't do that without you."

"Then it's a good thing you don't have to."

Lee took a deep breath, stepped forward and reached for something he knew he didn't really deserve; Megan's hand. He smiled nervously and hoped she'd accept his proposal.

24. The Best View In The World

So many times over the last couple of years, Zara had taken the time, two hours at least, to walk Toffee up Portsdown Hill. She did so at least once a week whenever her husband was away and always paused at the top to take in the wonderful view. As she did, she always imagined what Jayden was looking at. He was in the navy, so like her it was often the sea. Sometimes nothing but that, sometimes a boring functional port or exotic Caribbean island.

Often he'd email Zara pictures of places he visited. Sometimes he sent postcards. Always he'd tell her what he'd seen and done, by text, phone call or in person when he returned.

Before they'd moved near Portsmouth, Zara and Toffee's regular walks were in areas well known to Jayden, so she'd had no need to describe them. The view from Portsdown Hill was new to him. They had been there together, but only in the car and not really to see the view. Once they'd watched fireworks, but naturally it was dark and the colourful explosions eclipsed the city lights.

Zara noted small details to tell Jayden about. '*I saw wild orchids today*,' she'd text. Or, '*there were people flying kites, I might try that.*'

The bigger picture included the city of Portsmouth, the Isle of Wight and The Solent between them. The sea might be a calm blue reflection of a cloudless sky, green and studded with white horses, or so dark it seemed bottomless. Zara saw yacht races, cruise ships drift serenely past and occasionally her husband's ship sailing in.

"It's the best view in the world," she told Jayden.

When he was home he teased her a little, by suggesting other places to walk Toffee. "I don't want to go up Portsdown Hill yet – I'm saving the best until last!"

It wasn't a problem. Zara was happy walking along the seafront with him, or through the rose gardens at Southsea, or getting in the car and visiting the New Forest. Toffee was even more easily pleased – having both his humans home was enough excitement, even if they just walked him down the shop for a pint of milk or threw a ball in the garden.

Once he'd retired from the navy Jayden said, "After sailing the seven seas I finally have time to properly appreciate the best view in the world for myself."

Over his years in the navy Jayden had seen fascinating sea creatures, moored within sight of Sydney Opera House, or been surrounded by ice. He'd helped in rescue missions, defended coastlines and taken part in international operations.

"You might be disappointed after all the amazing things you've seen," Zara said.

"Somehow I doubt it."

They set off quite early. The sun hadn't yet burned through the morning mist. The dull boom of ship's foghorns seemed to follow them as they climbed.

"I don't suppose you enjoy that sound," Zara said. "But I find it comforting. It reminded me that there were safety precautions helping to ensure you come back to me."

"There are more pleasant sounds to hear on a ship," Jayden told her. "A pipe to say there's mail to be collected or that we can go ashore, especially when we're back in Portsmouth and I know you'll be waiting for me on the jetty."

Toffee, as usual, was torn between racing ahead after the

rabbits he hadn't a hope of catching, and staying with Zara and Jayden. Due to talking over plans, watching Toffee, and paying attention to where they placed their feet on the steep and slippery path, they didn't realise the early morning mist had become quite dense fog. That was not until they reached the spot where Zara always stopped to look.

Below them, in every direction, was nothing but swirling white.

Jayden turned to Zara and smiled. "The best view in the world," he said.

"Not exactly. Much as I love it when there's actually something to see, that's not what I meant when I said it was the best view in the world. That was the sight of your ship coming into harbour. I knew as soon as Toffee and I had walked home it would be time to come and meet you. All this," she gestured into the mist, "isn't the best view in the world."

"You're right, it isn't, nor anything I've seen while I've been away." He gently held her face in his hands. "This right here, you smiling at me, that's the best view in the world."

Thank you for reading this book. I hope you enjoyed it. If you did, I'd really appreciate it if you could leave a short review on Amazon and/or Goodreads.

To learn more about my writing life, hear about new releases and get a free short story, sign up to my newsletter – https://mailchi.mp/677f65e1ee8f/sign-up or you can find the link on my website patsycollins.uk

More books by Patsy Collins

Novels –

Firestarter
Escape To The Country
A Year And A Day
Paint Me A Picture
Leave Nothing But Footprints

Non-fiction –

From Story Idea To Reader
(co-written with Rosemary J. Kind)

A Year Of Ideas:
365 sets of writing prompts and exercises

Short story collections –

Over The Garden Fence
Up The Garden Path
Through The Garden Gate
In The Garden Air

No Family Secrets
Can't Choose Your Family
Keep It In The Family
Family Feeling
Happy Families

All That Love Stuff
With Love And Kisses
Lots Of Love

Slightly Spooky Stories I
Slightly Spooky Stories II
Slightly Spooky Stories III
Slightly Spooky Stories IV

Just A Job
Perfect Timing
A Way With Words
Dressed To Impress
Coffee & Cake
Not A Drop To Drink

Printed in Great Britain
by Amazon

65838836R00088